NICOLA GRIFFITH

Winner of the

Otherwise (formerly James Tiptree Jr.) Award

Lambda Literary Award

Premio Italia

Nebula Award

Washington State Book Award

Society of Authors ADCI Literary Prize

Los Angeles Times Book Prize

and World Fantasy Award

"Ms. Griffith is an astonishingly gifted writer. . . . Her work is of the very best in the lesbian and gay literary field."
—Allen Ginsberg

"Nicola Griffith's prose is beautiful in every sense of the word."
—April Adams, *The Lesbian Review*

"Brutal, unsparing . . . full of power and healing."
—Joanne Rixon, *Seattle Times* review of *So Lucky*

"A knockout!"
—Ursula K. Le Guin, on *Ammonite*

"A classic for the ages."
—Karen Rought, Subjectify Media, on *Spear*

"*Hild* is a world built fiber by fiber from the ground up, immersive as a river in rain."
—Amal El-Mohtar, NPR, on *Hild*

"With its persuasive characters trying to form identities in an unstable society, its midnight streets and shabby apartments, and its vast industrial engines, *Slow River* is a powerful prose poem on issues that are already with us."
—Gary Wolfe, *Locus*

"In Griffith's hands, a conversation . . . is as thrilling as a spear thrust through a man's cheek."
—Nicole Rudick, *New York Review of Books*, on *Menewood*

PM PRESS OUTSPOKEN AUTHORS SERIES

1. *The Left Left Behind*
   Terry Bisson
2. *The Lucky Strike*
   Kim Stanley Robinson
3. *The Underbelly*
   Gary Phillips
4. *Mammoths of the Great Plains*
   Eleanor Arnason
5. *Modem Times 2.0*
   Michael Moorcock
6. *The Wild Girls*
   Ursula K. Le Guin
7. *Surfing the Gnarl*
   Rudy Rucker
8. *The Great Big Beautiful Tomorrow*
   Cory Doctorow
9. *Report from Planet Midnight*
   Nalo Hopkinson
10. *The Human Front*
    Ken MacLeod
11. *New Taboos*
    John Shirley
12. *The Science of Herself*
    Karen Joy Fowler
13. *Raising Hell*
    Norman Spinrad
14. *Patty Hearst & The Twinkie Murders: A Tale of Two Trials*
    Paul Krassner
15. *My Life, My Body*
    Marge Piercy
16. *Gypsy*
    Carter Scholz
17. *Miracles Ain't What They Used to Be*
    Joe R. Lansdale
18. *Fire.*
    Elizabeth Hand
19. *Totalitopia*
    John Crowley
20. *The Atheist in the Attic*
    Samuel R. Delany
21. *Thoreau's Microscope*
    Michael Blumlein
22. *The Beatrix Gates*
    Rachel Pollack
23. *A City Made of Words*
    Paul Park
24. *Talk like a Man*
    Nisi Shawl
25. *Big Girl*
    Meg Elison
26. *The Planetbreaker's Son*
    Nick Mamatas
27. *The First Law of Thermodynamics*
    James Patrick Kelly
28. *Utopias of the Third Kind*
    Vandana Singh
29. *Night Shift*
    Eileen Gunn
30. *The Collapsing Frontier*
    Jonathan Lethem

31. *The Presidential Papers*
John Kessel

32. *The Last Coward on Earth*
Cara Hoffman

33. *Not What I Intended*
Nancy Kress

34 *She Is Here*
Nicola Griffith

35 *Veni Vidi Venti*
Ian Shoales

36 *The Tongue I Dream In*
Sheree Renée Thomas

37. *Machine Elves Descending*
John King

37 *FLUME*
Brian Evenson

38 *The History of the Decline and Fall of the Galactic Empire*
Toh EnJoe

SHE IS HERE

Nicola Griffith

PM PRESS | 2026

Editor's note: The author of this volume prefers British spelling, so this is reflected in its text.

"A Writer's Manifesto" was first published in Ask Nicola (an early blog), December 13, 2011.
"Overwriting the Old Story" was first published (as "Rewriting the Old Disability Script") in the *New York Times*, November 14, 2018.
"Branding: It Burns" was first published in *The Weeklings*, 2014.
"Wife" was first published on nicolagriffith.com, June 23, 2014.
"My Story, Mystery" was first published in the *Los Angeles Review of Books*, September 10, 2015.
"The Women You Didn't See" was first published the *Los Angeles Review of Books*, July 2015, and appeared soon after in *Letters to Tiptree*, edited by Alexandra Pierce and Alisa Krasnostein, August 2015.
"Glimmer" was first published in the anthology *Particulates*, edited by Nalo Hopkinson, in 2018.
"Cold Wind" was first published in *Tor.com/Reactor Magazine*, April 16, 2014.
"Down the Path of the Sun" was first published in *Interzone* #34, March/April 1990, and has been reprinted many times since.
"Iceberg," "Crippled Body," "Love-Hate," "Thief," and "Many Things in Dumnet" appear in print for the first time in this volume.

She Is Here

ISBN (paperback): 979-8-88744-149-8
ISBN (e-book): 979-8-88744-150-4
LCCN: 2025935974

Series editors: Nisi Shawl and Nick Mamatas
Cover design by John Yates/www.stealworks.com
Author photo by Kelley Eskridge
Insides by Jonathan Rowland

10 9 8 7 6 5 4 3 2 1

Printed in the USA

CONTENTS

NONFICTION
A Writer's Manifesto 1
Overwriting the Old Story 2
Branding: It Burns 6
Wife 15
My Story, Mystery: A Letter to Hild of Whitby 19
The Women You Didn't See: A Letter to Alice Sheldon 32

DRAWING: GRIFFIN, MAYBE 40

POETRY
Iceberg 41
Crippled Body 42
Love-Hate 43
Thief 44

DRAWING: KING BIRD 45

FICTION
Glimmer 46
Cold Wind 50
Down the Path of the Sun 62
Many Things in Dumnet 76

DRAWING: HAPPY HOUND 132

"Otherwise Unremarkable" 133
Nicola Griffith interviewed by Nisi Shawl

About the Author 149

For Kelley, who lights my way home

A Writer's Manifesto

When I write, dear reader, I don't want to build a careful tale for you to discuss with a smile in a sunny place. I want to own you. I don't want to be The New Hit Series, I want to be pornography: to thrill you so hard you're ashamed but can't help yourself crawling back for more.

I want to write a novel that invades you. I want to control what you think and feel, to put you right there, right then, killing and being killed, fucking and being fucked, cooking and starving, drinking and thinking, barely surviving and absolutely thriving. I want to give you a life you've never had and change the one you live.

How? I will take control of your mirror neurons. I will give you tastes and textures, torments and terrain you might never find in your real life. I will take you, sweep you off your feet, own you. For a while. For a while when you're lost in my book you will be somewhere else, somewhen else, someone else.

I control the horizontal, I control the vertical. Sit back, relax, enjoy. When you're done, take a breath, have a smoke, figure out who you are now, and come back for more.

Overwriting the Old Story

Implicit bias and socialisation are processes reliant on story: story that conditions us to feel, think, and behave in ways generally approved of by those around us. Although often invisible to us, this conditioning or bias constrains and guides our behaviour—but it can be changed when we learn to see the old, embedded story and then find a new and better story to overwrite it.

I am a queer, disabled writer who grew up Catholic in the north of England. Some of the stories I was told about who I was and my place in the world were visible to me; some were not.

I grew up at the fulcrum of two competing stories. In Yorkshire, even more than four hundred years after the reign of Henry VIII, Catholics were a small, feared, and embattled minority—to the point of being spat upon in the street. To my family, friends, and teachers (mostly nuns) Catholics were Good, the Norm. Out on the street and to our neighbours, Catholics were Bad, Other. Perhaps that awareness of duelling narratives was what inoculated me against other cultural stories.

I knew when I was four years old that I was girl who liked other girls, and it seemed perfectly natural to me. I knew I was amazing, and that if I fancied girls then fancying girls must be amazing. No one thought to talk about sexuality to a four-year-old, so for several years my story was the only story I knew about it. It wasn't until I was nine or so that I found out that the dominant story—as told by family, church, school, neighbours, and books such as *The Well of Loneliness*—was that queerness was Bad. By then it was easy to counterprogramme anti-lesbian bias with my own, better story; I did not develop internalised homophobia. (My two queer sisters did not have such overweening self-esteem; they were not so lucky. They died young.)

When I was fifteen, I went with my girlfriend to a gay club where, for the first time, I saw two men kissing. I felt instant and visceral revulsion. I had spent the last ten years counter-programming anti-lesbian hate but hadn't thought to do the same for gay men; I had had no countervailing story.

I was appalled. And felt ridiculous: a homophobic lesbian. I was determined to change, and I could: I now had access to a different story. I went back to the club night after night for a month until that new story—this is what some men do; it's normal—overwrote the old.

The novels I write come from who I am, where I am, emotionally and physically. The protagonists of my novels are queer women, and because I've never associated being queer with emotional struggle, my characters' bodies are sites of delight rather than difficulty. The protagonists are queer, but the story isn't about being queer because, to me, queerness is an old story, long sorted.

But disability was different.

I did not grow up disabled. I did not develop an awareness of this culture's bias against, horror at, and disdain for physical and intellectual difference. No one explicitly told me that disability was bad; they didn't have to. The bias was pervasive and implicit. I did not learn to defend against or counterprogramme that ableist story. Instead, I absorbed and internalised it.

I was diagnosed with MS over thirty years ago. Perhaps because my physical impairments gained on me slowly, it took me years to feel the sting of nondisabled people's dismissal. It took me years to begin to understand that I had been dismissing my disabled self. It took me years to recognise the ableist narrative I'd absorbed, because I had nothing to contradict it.

As a child, I saw no disabled women—queer or otherwise—in real life or on page or screen. When disabled characters finally began to appear in books and on screen, they were distorted clichés: tragic cripples, angry cripples, helpless cripples. Cripples whose bodies were portrayed as sites of struggle and despair, reflecting "how awful it would be to be disabled." Stories written by the nondisabled who reinforced the ableist narrative because that's all they knew.

Imagine if all queer fiction today were still as miserable as *The Well of Loneliness*. Then imagine that most disability fiction is worse.

Actually, you don't have to imagine. In 2017, disabled poet and memoirist Kenny Fries formulated a test for disability in fiction. It's based on the Bechdel Test (which asks whether a work of fiction features at least two women who talk to each other about something other than a man). Fries asked, "Does a work have more than one disabled character? Do the disabled characters have their own narrative purpose other than the education and profit of a nondisabled character? Is the character's disability not eradicated either by curing or killing?"[1]

The Fries Test is a low bar. In order to pass, a novel's disabled characters do not have to have names, or talk to each other at all, never mind about something other than disability. Nonetheless, in late 2017 I put out a call on social media for book-length fiction

1 Kenny Fries, "The Fries Test: On Disability Representation in Our Culture," *Medium*, November 1, 2017, https://medium.com/@kennyfries/the-fries-test-on-disability-representation-in-our-culture-9d1bad72cc00.

for adults that might pass the test. After many months, and input from hundreds of readers, I had a list of just over fifty titles. Of these fifty, some were old, some out of print, and a handful not in English.

This was a shocking result. According to the Stanford Literary Lab, at that time there were about five million novels extant in English. According to US and UK Census data, about one in five people are disabled. In order for stories that pass the Fries Test—that is, to offer at least a reasonable chance of not being ableist narratives—to represent the experience and reality of UK and US residents, the number of novels on my list should be one million.

One million. And we had fifty.

Think about all those stories that are missing. Stories that we need to overwrite the corrosive narrative of ableism. Without those stories, the implicit bias will continue and the cycle will renew itself endlessly. We changed queer literature, and the world, with story. We can do it again. First we need to write those stories in our own voices, our strong, beautiful, ordinary, disabled voices.

Branding: It Burns

Being an explanation of why for novelists the notion of branding is fraught with peril

When branding guru Wally Olins died, an *Economist* review of his posthumous *Brand New: The Shape of Brands to Come* (Thames & Hudson, 2014), quoted his assertion that branding is "about knowing who you are . . . and showing it."

It sounds simple; for a novelist it is not.

Writing is both a verb and a noun, a process and a product. The job of a writer is staged: creating then selling, that is, art then commerce. Stepping from one mode to the other involves a profound rearrangement, a state change, as I found out on US publication of my novel *Hild*.

#

To learn to create the kind of novel I aim for—to conjure another time and place with the authority to immerse a reader—to run my software on the readers' hardware—took years of two different and contradictory practices: disciplined focus on craft, and a kind of unmoored wandering to find my voice.

Basic craft isn't too hard: if you have the instincts, any competent teacher and/or editor can help you hone them.[1] To reach a more expert level, though, requires personal study, and work, lots of work. The only way to learn a novelist's craft is by doing; by doing over and over until it feels exactly right. There are no shortcuts. There might be times, yes, when we write on our own bow wave, when we conjure a brilliant story or novel from thin air without much experience, but the trick is being able to do it again. And again. And to understand why something works, or why it doesn't—and how to fix it. Eventually we understand our tools so well that we know immediately if an idea is worth trying to capture or not.

It's expert-level craft that creates the conditions for immersive fiction: the ability to trigger a reader's mirror neurons.[2] When I immerse a reader, they live inside a character for a while; they not only see what my character sees but smell the rain-wet hair, hear the suck of mud under her horse's hoof, and feel the catch in her mount's gait. They think her thoughts, and learn her lessons; they dream her dreams, just for a little while.

But all the craft on the planet won't take the reader there unless the writer has been there first, unless the writer understands the character and her world so well it has become a kind of felt experience. Research isn't enough. Research alone leads to regurgitated passages in novels so superficially digested that readers[3] can see the bones of the original distorting the story.

1 Sadly, I suspect that the incompetent outnumber the competent.

2 A mirror neuron is a neuron that fires both when we act and when we see someone else perform the same act. Mirror neurons are found in the premotor cortex, the supplementary motor area, the primary somatosensory cortex and the inferior parietal cortex. The mirror neuron system is what helps us understand the actions and intentions of other people; to recreate others' experience inside ourselves. Some argue it is the foundation of empathy.

3 Guilty. I could name the (unacknowledged) sources of more than one bestselling historical novelist.

If they were immersed at all—a big if—that doesn't last. True immersion requires far more than the authority of researched detail; it demands a kind of indwelling. Writers must know their imaginary time, place, and people: the light, the smell, the texture. We must know it as lived experience to understand muscles sore from warping the loom with wool we've spun and carded and dyed, sheared from sheep we've raised and bred, on hills we own.

The writer must find a still, quiet place, one free of distraction.[4] It's only from that place, real or metaphorical, that she can dwell inside her creation, or wander to find her next.

The writer as artist is a kind of shaman: we explore unknown territory and bring back maps. There's no training course and no useful certificate;[5] we have to find our own voice, our own path. And the path for every novelist—and every novel—is different. It is not signposted (because if it's been visited many times before it's not art but cliché, which is not our business here). We have to wander before we find the path, and then climb the path alone. Every new novel is a journey; every new journey a risk.

Writing *Hild* was the biggest risk I've ever taken as a novelist. For a variety of reasons it felt impossible.[6] In the end I had to simply begin: leap into the void in the hope that my words would catch me. They did, they always do, but the book wouldn't be what it is without hurling myself into the unknown without

---

4 It doesn't have to be literally quiet—in an urban setting that's sometimes asking the impossible—but it does have to be isolated in terms of other people for predictable periods. Without the app Freedom, for example, *Hild* would never have been written.

5 MFAs are useful for two things: being paid/supported while you practice your craft, and proving that you can teach others to get an MFA.

6 I talk about some of them in "My Story, Mystery."

distraction. In other words, writing a novel is a risk that demands a particular freedom: I can't leap until I am untethered.

Adrienne Rich, in "When We Dead Awaken: Writing as Re-Vision," wrote:

> For a poem to coalesce . . . there has to be an imaginative transformation of reality which is in no way passive. And a certain freedom of the mind is needed, freedom to press on, to enter the currents of your thought like a glider pilot, knowing that your motion can be sustained, that the buoyancy of your attention will not be suddenly snatched away. . . . You have to be free to play. . . . For writing is renaming.[7]

To support writing, the process of creating the product for sale, a writer must feel unfettered. We can't afford to be bound by what has gone before—even our own work. But to support the novel itself, the publication and sale of the product, a writer needs another skill set entirely.

#

Hild is a novel set in seventh-century Britain. It is not a fantasy; the eponymous main character lived fourteen hundred years ago; she was real. In my version of her early life, she is not a lesbian. Yet the first review of the book begins, "LGBT scifi writer Nicola Griffith . . ."[8] And another refers to "lesbian fantasy and crime

---

7 Adrienne Rich, *On Lies, Secrets, and Silence: Selected Prose 1966–1978* (W.W. Norton, 1979), 33–50

8 I'm still puzzled over my apparent multiplicity: I am lesbian and gay and bisexual and trans all at the same time.

writer Nicola Griffith." In other words, what was being reviewed was not the book at hand, but me, the author, and my previous novels.[9] The book and I were being labelled Genre/Queer, branded as Other.[10]

Branded. It's a brutal word for a brutal practice: a label burned into the hide without permission. On a cow, a brand marks an animal that belongs to a herd. Yet to create art the artist must be as free as possible from the herd mentality: neither belong to any group nor follow any but our own particular, often peculiar path.

So how do I counteract the influence of others' perception of *Where I've been* on *Where I'm going*? Is it even possible?

#

As a writer my ultimate consumer, my target audience if you like,[11] is the reader. Not immediately, of course. These days, generally speaking, when a writer finishes her first book, her initial audience is a potential agent. Once she's found her agent, the agent helps her find an editor/publisher. The publisher then finds the right media editors/producers to help spread the word—but it's not the writer's job to go after them, it's the publicist's. The writer's job is to go after readers.

---

9 None of which—this was before *Spear*—was fantasy.

10 The further outside the perceived Norm—which in literary terms is cis, straight, white, male, middle-class—we as a writer live, the more firmly we and our work are nailed to a category, expected to appeal only to readers who themselves belong to that category. I have a trinity of nails: a woman who writes about women who love women. To make matters worse, my protagonists tend to have agency—not always a popular stance with critics when they are used to equating Other with Victim.

11 I'm not sure I do. A target is something you hit. A brand is a deep mark, most usually a burn scar, applied to chattel.

But long before she can get to the readers, she will be asked—by one or all of those agents, editors, publicists—about the size of her platform: If she has a newsletter or podcast, how many subscribers? If she's on Bluesky/Threads/Instagram/TikTok/Mastodon (and she'd better be on some or all of them), how many followers does she have?

I'm lucky. I've been interacting with readers since the Ask Nicola[12] feature of my first website over twenty-five years ago. And I've had the same editor for five of my novels (though at three different houses). No one needed to ask if I was comfortable and competent with social media. The publication of *Hild*, I thought, would not be hard or different.

#

In terms of communication, the primary job of a novelist is to talk to readers. This job begins and ends with the book. Given that readers are, essentially, consumers, and, according to Olin, "consumers crave 'authenticity,'" if the novelist wants to speak to her readers outside the confines of her book using, say, social media, she needs to tell a story about herself on social media that matches the story she tells the publicists. The publicists in turn tell media producers a story about her/her novel that ideally matches the story she is telling her followers on social media.

You see where this is going?

Reputation and identity, Olin tells us, have similar meanings. Oh yes. In order to publish books we have to prove that we can sell books. To sell books we have to tell a story about them: we have to brand them. We have to build them an identity. We have to build ourselves a reputation. In so doing, we brand ourselves. That's part

12 Now a healthy blog.

of what hurts: it's we who drive ourselves into the cattle chute, we who pick up the glowing iron, we who burn the label deep into our hide. We scar ourselves.

#

Carolyn Buck Luce, a partner at EY, which until 2013 was Ernst & Young (I'm guessing a brand consultant advised them to change), tells Sylvia Ann Hewlett in *Executive Presence*:[13] "You've got to have the vision and write the path. It's your responsibility to figure out how to align your talents and gifts to the culture so that, long-term, you achieve your goals. When you are the curator of your authenticity, you can invest intentionally—and then it's a win-win for you and your company."

Here she is talking about aligning with specific corporate cultures rather than art. Corporate culture likes to align itself with corporate values, which in turn support the corporate mission. In other words, people who work for a company are supposed to believe in what the company is trying to do, and the way that they do it. They may have a wonderful vision, fabulous talents, but if they don't fit, they don't belong and will eventually be unsuccessful.

Whatever other goals a corporation might hold, one thing it must always do, particularly if it is publicly held, is to make money. Much corporate moneymaking is about market share: fighting to take a bigger slice of the pie than rival corporations.

Publishers are corporations. It's in their interest to sell as many books as possible. Art might be what lies between the covers of the

13 Perhaps Hewett would not characterize it this way, but it seems like an executive-level self-help book on personal branding: how to build a reputation portable between corporate jobs.

book, and might be its potential for speaking to those who read it, but it's commerce that gets that book into the hands of readers.

Novelists are expected to get behind the book and push. I prepared.

Hild's publication took me by surprise. Buzz began much earlier and lasted much longer than I'd anticipated. I enjoyed it at first. Then I began to feel increasingly uncomfortable blowing my own horn, talking about myself and my book all the time: the notices and reviews, the honours and appearances, the interviews and photos. It didn't fit my need to also move unnoticed through a crowd, to observe, to roam freely. I wanted to vanish back into creation mode.

However, a combination of unforeseeable factors[14] meant I didn't have much else to discuss that was relevant to my book, engaging, and uplifting enough to boost sales/my brand. So I talked grimly on.

#

A writer spends a lot of time on a high wire strung between art and commerce. Sometimes we lose our balance.

Writers are not corporations; it is not our job to fight to take slices of pie from other writers. Perhaps that's what our publishers believe is our job but I disagree. Our job, as artists, as creators, is to create art so delicious, so sustaining, that readers are hungry for more. Our job is to *grow the pie.*

In my late teens I read that Sarah Orne Jewett, a nineteenth-century American novelist, used to spend six months of the year isolated in the countryside, writing. Then she would come to

14 My health, which essentially kept me on heavy doses of opioids and pinned to a chair for six months.

town for months to be sociable, to mingle, support the book, drink her fill of people. Then back to the glorious freedom of unconnectedness and dreaming, wandering until she found the path, and climbing it. I have been longing for something similar ever since: to spend half the year free to think in seventh-century metaphors and dream in the poetry of Old English. I want time to wander into unmapped territory.

It will have to wait. I have planes to catch, interviews to give, blog posts to write and feeds to maintain. And in many ways I love it; I love talking to my readers. It's why writing-as-product distracts me so much from writing-as-process. Creating, wandering those wild crags, is exhilarating, but it can be daunting, too. Being with the herd sometimes feels easier.

If I have learnt any lesson from the publication of *Hild* it is: make sure publication on both sides of the Atlantic is synchronous and seamless. Get all the sociable marketing and support done at the same time. And then come home, turn off Wi-Fi, and let the phone battery die. Roam free.

Wife

Two and half months before the publication of *Hild*, I emailed my editor at Farrar, Straus and Giroux: "I hope it's not too late to change my author bio. I no longer want it to read that I'm Kelley's 'partner' because we're getting married."

He wrote back: "No problem. I'll just change *partner* to *wife*. So the end of the bio will read 'She lives in Seattle with her wife, the writer Kelley Eskridge.'"

I blinked. I blinked again. I hesitated. *Wife*. Then (with some misgivings) I gave the okay.

Twenty years earlier, when I first married Kelley, in a ceremony with zero legal validity but much emotional power, in front of family and friends who'd flown in from all over the world, I might have hurt anyone who called me *her wife* or her *my wife*.

But when we got married on the twentieth anniversary of that first wedding, in front of a judge, with the full legal force of the USA and UK and many other countries behind our vows, we used the word *wife*. We'd talked about it over the years. We'd disliked it over the years. But when we were looking at the old, old vow "to take this woman as your legally wedded wife" with all the ancient rhythms of have and hold, richer and poorer, sickness and in health we knew it was the right word.

Yet it's still not easy to introduce Kelley as *my wife*.

I read my first feminist theory when I was nineteen. It made me so angry that I couldn't leave my flat for three days because I thought I might hurt the first man I saw. In the countries I call home (the UK and US), until relatively recently husbands could rape their wives with impunity. Wives could do nothing about that. A wife belonged to her husband. A wife submitted to him and depended upon him; a wife wasn't allowed to make decisions for herself, to borrow money . . .

So, growing up, *wife* was, to me, an ugly word. Anathema. A badge of second-class citizenship. So ugly, in fact, that it changed the way I thought. I and the woman I first lived with and loved[1] never called each other my anything. Not even my lover. Using the possessive for another human being seemed wholly wrong.

And then I met Kelley and fell in love. And now she is my wife. Now I am her wife. What changed?

The etymology of *wife* is complicated. Looked at superficially we can say the Modern English *wife* (female spouse) is from Middle English (ME) *wif*/ *wiif*/*wyf* (mistress of a household) which in turn is from Old English (OE) *wīf* (female, lady, woman—from *wīfman*, female person, though I'm not sure when that formulation occurred). But look a little deeper and you see that various meanings from past eras hang on in different guises, so we get the OE sense of woman preserved in *midwife* and *old wife's tale*, and the ME sense in *housewife* and (more specialised) *fishwife* (tradeswoman of humble rank).

And then we ask, where did *wīf* come from? From Proto-Germanic **wiban*.[2] Which in turns might (things apparently get a

---

1 But see how awkward that phrasing is?

2 This disquisition is from notes I jotted down some time ago without attribution. (It's a bad habit I'm trying to break.) A quick search shows that a good chunk comes from the Online Etymology Dictionary but some, well, it's a bit of mystery. I'm guessing I consulted the

bit guessy at this altitude, or maybe depth) come from the Proto-Indo-European **weip-* (to twist, turn, wrap, perhaps with a sense of veiled person), or **ghwibh-* (shame, also pudenda). So: wife might ultimately come from a sense of hiding one's shame. No wonder I've never liked it.

But words change. They change because the world does, because the speakers of a language put the words to different use, one that reflects their evolving worldview. In this sense, frothing conservatives are right: changing the traditional definition of marriage has changed marriage.

When two women call each other *wife*, wife no longer means chattel. It can't—chattel can't own each other. *Wife* no longer means object-not-subject, that is, subject to another's will. How can two people with the same status subject each other to anything? These days, in the US and UK, *wife* means *woman in a legal marriage*. By association, woman also no longer means object-not-subject. It no longer carries with it the implication that someone else is in charge. A woman is no longer automatically a lesser member of a household. Wives and husbands,[3] women and men, are both now human beings in and of themselves—though legally related. Family. Which entails obligation and connection, a belonging that isn't necessarily possessive. I never had a problem calling the woman who bore me my mother, though no one would

---

Oxford English Dictionary, my favourite book, and that I added two and two myself to make four, but if anyone out there recognises any of it, please let me know. I'll be happy to give credit. Oh, and the asterisk is an academic/linguistic convention denoting a certain amount of back-formation/extrapolation—or, as you or I might put it, guessing.

3 Husband is a later formulation. It's from Old Norse and probably replaced OE *wer* in the thirteenth century.

have dreamt of assuming she was my chattel. Rather, we belonged to each other.

More women—of every age and sexuality and marital status—understand this and are refusing to accept the notion that women belong to men. I don't think it's a coincidence, for example, that the Twitter hashtag #YesAllWomen began sometime after the SCOTUS ruling on marriage equality. Yes, before that there was #bindersfullofwomen. And, yes, SCOTUS ruled as it did because attitudes were already changing. But they are part of a continuum.

Interesting times lie ahead.

My Story, Mystery: A Letter to Hild of Whitby

Dear Hild,

You were magnificent, I think, but hidden: a black hole at the heart of history. We can trace you only by your gravitational pull. We know, for example, that the very first piece of English literature was forged in the fire of your influence;[1] that in the so-called Dark Ages[2] you built and ran Whitby Abbey, the foundation at the centre of what became Northumbria's Golden Age. There you hosted and facilitated the meeting of kings, princes, and bishops that changed Britain, the Synod of Whitby. But we have no account of you beyond a five-page sketch in a 1,300-year-old history, most of which recites the standard hagiographic miracles and visions of the time. We have no gossipy Life, no scholarly monograph, no racy romance cycle. There isn't even a grave.

#

1 "Cædmon's Hymn," the earliest extant example of Old English vernacular poetry. For a discussion of what that means, exactly, a good place to begin is *Double Agents* by Clare A. Lees and Gillian R. Overing (University of Pennsylvania Press, 2001).

2 These days the preferred term is Early Medieval, though some might argue for Late Antiquity or the Migration Age, depending on geographical location or area of interest.

Whitby Abbey[3] is now a ruin overlooking a harbour on the northeast coast of Yorkshire less than two hours' drive from where I was born. It's visible for miles, from land and sea. On a summer day, the clifftop ruins are lovely, but northern summers are brief, and when the sun isn't shining it's impossible to ignore the winds that howl in off the North Sea. What prompted you to choose such an exposed spot? Vanity, asceticism, a craving for God's presence? I doubt it. I think the sea itself was the point.[4]

The poetry of your era is full of voyages.[5] Anglo-Saxons were born sailors. For you, the sea was not a wilderness or a barrier but a road—one less treacherous than the broken remains of those built by Romans. Roman roads were a marvel: cutting through mountains, slicing across valleys, soaring over rivers. They were monumental, implacable. But not indestructible. When Roman military power withdrew, administrative structures failed. Without taxes, regular maintenance ceased. Trees grew, bridges fell, and ditches clogged. Marsh reclaimed great stretches; locals took beautifully trimmed mile markers, bridge footings, and foundation pavers to shore up walls or use as post-foundations. As

3 Hild would have called it Streonæshalch. The current ruins are that of a Benedictine monastery founded in the late eleventh century on the ruins of Hild's foundation. There's been a lot of coastal erosion; indications are that at least part of Streonæshalch—or what was left of it after the Vikings destroyed it in the ninth century—lies beneath the waves. ("Whitby" is a Viking name.)

4 New archaeological evidence indicates that although today's ruins are built more or less in the same spot as Hild's original foundation, as hundreds of meters of cliff have been lost to erosion the centre would then have been largely sheltered from the wind.

5 Poetry written down long after Hild's death, once an Old English literary tradition was well established. A tradition she may well have created.

the once-unified province broke into warring tribes, parts of any traveller's route ran through enemy territory.

It was quicker and easier to sail from Whitby to Bamburgh, the seat of Northumbrian royal power, than to ride. York and every other major Northumbrian centre was on a navigable river.

So the sea was the point; the sea and the harbour, one of the only havens on that stretch of coast, a place where a ship could pull in at night for travellers to rest, or to consult you. Travel was clearly one of your priorities: your ease of access to those in power—and theirs to you. Why? What made you so important? We don't know. We don't even know your full name.

#

Old English names are generally dithematic, built of two elements, a prefix and suffix. According to the only document that attests to your existence, Bede's *Historia ecclesiastica gens Anglorum (HE)*,[6] your mother was Breguswith, your father Hereric, and your sister—neatly—Hereswith. But you were just Hild, which means *battle*.[7] Bede was writing fifty years after you died; I doubt you met him, or

---

6 There's mention of Hild, too, in another document (the *Anglo-Saxon Chronicle*) but it adds nothing. But see Christine E. Fell, "Hild, Abbess of Streonæshalch" in *Hagiography and Medieval Literature: A Symposium*, ed. Hans Bekker-Nielsen, Peter Foote Jorgen Hojgaard Jorgensen and Tore Nyberg (Odense University Press, 1981) for discussion of a lost Life. There are a variety of translations of Bede. These days it's usual to interpret the title as *The Ecclesiastical History of the English People*. I first read it as *A History of the English Church and People*, translated by Leo Sherley-Price and revised by R.E. Latham (Penguin, 1968). All translations are from that revised and reprinted 1968 edition, unless otherwise specified.

7 There is some scholarly debate about what the rest might have been: Hildeswith? Hildeburh? (I like the latter: battle fortress.)

would have liked him if you had. He was a monk, one of the first generations of English oblates, with a very particular idea of women. Royal virgins were acceptable; wives and mothers of especially pious kings might rate a mention. Most of the time, though, Bede's monarchs seemed to mate with the air. *HE* was the foundational text of English history, the model and exemplar of the genre for the next millennium and a half, and, in it, women barely exist.

You are an exception.

Even so, *HE*'s scant mentions of you consist mainly of lists of the (male) bishops and (mostly male) saints you trained, and the (male) monarchs you advised. Bede writes that your father was murdered in exile, and while you were in the womb your mother dreamt you would be the light of the world and lead the way for Britain. He gives no clue how you might have managed this. I suspect, in fact, that Breguswith's prophecy, which imbued you with a corona of singularity, was part of what made your achievements, your whole life, possible; it was the best protection a mother could give.

As the second daughter of an assassinated should-have-been king, you needed all the help you could get. You were probably homeless and hunted, almost certainly illiterate—everyone was—a child surviving among petty warlords. Bede says none of this, of course. In his text you are born (we don't know where, exactly) and glide invisibly through the world until you appear at age thirteen alongside the real subject of his narrative, your great-uncle the king (who may be the one who murdered your father; Bede is conspicuously silent on this point), with whom you were baptised in the first wave of Anglo-Saxon conversions north of the Humber.[8] Then you vanish again for twenty years.

8 "Anglo-Saxon" is a fraught term, carrying with it more than a whiff of white nationalism, which these days I try to avoid.

Twenty years. That's a big chunk of anyone's life. Who did you love, kill, nurture, bear, heal, persuade, or fight in that time? We'll never know. But those twenty years must have been a crucible because the person who emerged was extraordinary.

You reappear at thirty-three, recruited to the church by the founding Bishop of Lindisfarne, Aidan, an Irishman by way of Iona. Aidan went to some lengths to persuade you; he must have needed you. Bede, though, doesn't see fit to tell us why—nor why you said yes. You joined the nascent Northumbrian church and some years later founded Whitby Abbey, a double house—with women and men religious—which shortly became the jewel of the north. Archaeological finds indicate that Whitby was a hive of cultural production: goldsmithing, weaving, and, of course, books. Bede tells us you ran the place "with great energy," that kings and princes "used to come and ask [your] advice in their difficulties and took it,"[9] and that you were so revered that all called you Mother.[10]

Some time after Aidan's death, you brought together the overking of Britain, his son, and the cream of the northern ecclesiastical elite for the famous Synod where the fate of the English church was decided.[11] The overking spurned the so-called

9 Roy M. Liuzza interprets this line as "Her wisdom was so great that not only ordinary people, but even kings and princes sometimes asked for and received her advice." *Broadview Anthology of British Literature*, Vol. 1 (Broadview Press, 2006). But whichever translation you read, the gist is clear: Hild spoke, important people listened.

10 This makes Hild sound nurturing and kind. But you don't get to be renowned enough to be remembered all over the world fourteen hundred years later by being sweetness and light. Mother Theresa, for example, might have helped millions, but from what I can gather she was not a gentle soul.

11 Synod of Whitby, 664 CE. There are many chewy academic discussions of the event, but Wikipedia gives a reasonable overview.

Celtic church (centred at Lindisfarne) in favour of aligning with Rome. Reading between the lines (not your lines, of course, and not in your language—there was no written Old English at that point) it was you who brought together the factions, forging an amalgam of the best of both, mitigating Pauline misogyny with Celtic cultural egalitarianism.[12]

That gift, the ability to bring together competing cultures, is what made the early creation of Old English literature possible. Religion and literacy, both previously the province of the elite, met and mated with the vernacular artistic tradition because you made it happen. You told Cædmon, a cowherd, to use his song-making gift in your service to spread the word of God. He did. His song, his poem, "Cædmon's Hymn, "was written down in the vernacular, probably at your abbey, very likely at your instigation. You brought together different traditions, different ways of understanding the world, and made something new. In terms of English literature, at least, your mother's prophecy came true: you lit the way.

You yourself remain in shadow.

#

We tend to think of history as fact, but history is just moments that have come down to us, embroidered over the ages: stories. And women's stories are missing. In a recent issue of *The Paris Review*, Hilary Mantel said, of revising a draft of *A Place of Greater Safety* a dozen years after she had written it, "When I read my draft, I saw that the women were wallpaper. There had been no material. Today you would think, Well, I must invent some, then.

---

12 Pre-Roman, Late Iron Age British society was largely matrilocal and matrilineal: men from elsewhere married into the women's land-owning families.

At the time I hadn't seen the need—I hadn't thought the women interesting."[13]

Of course we don't seem interesting, because our interesting bits are missing. As Virginia Woolf said:

> The history of England is the history of the male line, not of the female. . . . For very little is known about women. . . . Of our fathers we know always some fact, some distinction. They were soldiers or they were sailors; they filled that office or they made that law. But of our mothers, our grandmothers, our great-grandmothers, what remains? Nothing but a tradition. One was beautiful; one was red-haired; one was kissed by a Queen. We know nothing of them except their names and the dates of their marriages, and the number of children they bore.[14]

You are remembered as a woman so revered everyone called you Mother, but we don't know if you had children of your own, the colour of your hair, or the names of anyone you kissed. We have two legends: that the ammonites[15] that are found in such plenty at Whitby are the snakes you turned to stone, and seagulls dip their wings over the cliffs in your memory. The rest is a mystery.

#

---

13 Interview by Mona Simpson, "Hilary Mantel, The Art of Fiction No. 226," *The Paris Review* no. 212 (Spring 2015): 49.

14 Virginia Woolf, "Women and Fiction," *The Forum* 81, no. 2 (March 1929): 179.

15 The genus of ammonite found at Whitby is *Hildoceras bifrons*. In fact the whole family of ammonites is known as the *Hildoceratidae*.

> *his story*
> *history*
> *my story*
> *mystery*
> (Adele Aldridge, *Black Maria 1, no. 1, 1972)*

Stories help us empathise.[16] Without them, we lose sight of who we can be. Elena Ferrante says, "I wouldn't recognise myself without women's struggles, women's nonfiction, women's literature—they made me an adult."[17]

Without stories of women with power and agency, women like you, we don't see our shape and heft in the world or our own possibilities. We are poorer for it. We have no pictures of you, and no grave, but Whitby is built in your image and is your monument: elemental, unmistakable, arresting. It and you changed my life.

Yorkshire has been settled for thousands of years. Everywhere one turns there are the marks of human habitation: standing stones, Iron Age hillforts, Roman roads. The past is part of my landscape. I've danced katas in castles on mist-drenched mornings, daydreamed of Neolithic raiding parties on the moors, and hummed songs a Roman auxiliary's child might have learnt by Hadrian's Wall. But Whitby Abbey is unique. There the skin of the earth feels thin, the boundary between past and present transparent. Fossil plesiosaurs, like flying dragons that have crashed into the cliff in some alternate reality that might be running alongside our own, are freed from the rock every day

---

16 P. Matthijs Bal and Martijn Veltkamp, "How Does Fiction Reading Influence Empathy? An Experimental Investigation on the Role of Emotional Transportation," *PLOS One* 8, no. 1 (January 2013), https://pmc.ncbi.nlm.nih.gov/articles/PMC3559433/.

17 Interview by Sandro Ferri, "Elena Ferrante, The Art of Fiction No. 228," *The Paris Review* no. 212 (Spring 2015): 219.

by the tides; light shimmers over the sea like the first breath of the world; even the turf seems to tremble with immanence. To stand on the cliff at Whitby is to balance at the edge of reality. It was there that I understood the people from the past were real; at Whitby that I first wanted to know what it would be like to live in another time and place in another's skin. It was at Whitby Abbey, with a hand on those fallen stones, that I knew I would become a writer.

You made Whitby. On some level, you made me.

Of all the women remembered by history—even sketchily—you're the only one I know of who lived on her own terms. Your renown was not as anyone's parent or wife, or for suffering unspeakable torment or a martyr's death. All you achieved was as a person in your own right. You lived a long and successful life and died admired and powerful. You won.

You won. That single fact, that women can win, helped counterbalance all the nonsense I'd absorbed from history. Partly because I stood in those ruins and saw what you had made, I knew we could each triumph on our own terms and in our own service.

In a very real sense, then, I owe you everything. But I didn't want to write your story—your story as I'd first been taught it must have been.

#

History—his story—tells us that in the past, particularly so long ago, women lived narrow, caged lives: pawns of the marriage game, baby-making machines, handmaids of dynasty. The master story is that your constraints and those of your peers were terrible. But Bede tells us kings and princes travelled to you for advice—and took it. Somehow you must have remained outside the master story, but I could not see how.

The only way to find out how, to discover what made you who you were, was to write your story myself.

A paradox. To write a novel set in the Long Ago realistic enough, immersive enough, to persuade readers—who also grew up believing the master story—that this is how it was, this is who you were, yet that might appeal to those like me who have been taught to find women's roles in the past unbearably claustrophobic. It seemed impossible. Then I saw one faint and glimmering path.

If I could recreate the seventh century—a working world; its people, places, and web of political, religious, and personal relationships—I could then replay known events and watch what happened, see what shape a person with your achievements might take. But to feel confident that the you I imagined could have existed—for the experiment to be valid—I could not contravene what was known to be known, even in the smallest detail.

To even attempt such a thing was ridiculous. Intellectually, I knew this. But what keeps a writer going, what makes her able to think she will succeed where millions fail, is an almost psychotic self-belief. I'm guessing you had that too. However, to paraphrase Trollope, while the difficult can be done at once, the impossible takes a little longer.

It took me thirty years. For half that time, I didn't even know I was working my way into telling your story. My first novel, *Ammonite* (no, really, I didn't know), was set in the far future, my second in the near future, my next three, about a character named for Aud the Deepminded, a ninth-century Norwegian, then Irish queen, who founded Iceland (I still didn't know), set in the here and now. Some time after finishing the first Aud novel I started reading everything I could lay my hands on about the late sixth and early seventh century. Ethnography, archaeology, numismatics, jewellery, textiles, languages, food production, flora and fauna, weapons and warfare, medical approaches, religious belief—even the weather. I read a lot of poetry. Old English was foundational for me. I read several different translations of the extant poetry, then I read the originals (they come in a variety of recensions)—though I admit my understanding of the language is pitiful.

When I began to dream in the rhythms of heroic poetry, when I heard the shiver of new leaves in the wind and saw that shimmer of light over the sea, I was ready. And there you were, at the foot of an elm: three years old, wary, with a will of adamant. I fell for you, and I ached, because to get this right I could not flinch—there's no story, no growth and change, without struggle. And your name, after all, means battle.

#

When a novel is published these days it's part of the author's job to write publicity pieces to accompany the launch: lists, personal essays, travel-related features, anything which could plausibly relate to the work and might appeal to an editor or producer hungry for content. As *Hild* was to be reprinted as a UK paperback, I pondered what I could write to support it. The first thing I set about was a list, a Five Best essay for a national daily in which one talks about five novels that have influenced the work at hand.

It seemed easy. Five titles dropped into my head immediately: powerful, immersive novels set in a time, like yours, when wind and animal muscle powered the world, and life could be brutal. Each was an old friend, read and reread for decades. Three were by women and two by men; this proportion pleased me.

Then I realised that all, without exception, were about men. This disturbed me. These were the stories I loved, the historical fiction that had a powerful influence on my approach to writing;

stories of war and leadership, personal and political change, and great deeds. Stories of lives history tells us matters. Men's stories. I was appalled to see how the master story had influenced my own writing life.

I expanded the list of historical novels to ten, with the same result. It wasn't until I increased that number to twenty—this time including books set in much more recent times—that women began to pop up. I don't think it's a coincidence that every single one of these historical novels about women were created by women who identify as lesbian.

#

Did you love women, or men, or both (or neither)? We'll never know, and I doubt it mattered. But we all like to see ourselves mirrored in the world, so I chose to make you queer (not a word you would have understood).[18] The experience has brought—is still bringing—me vast joy. But, ah, I would give my big toe—perhaps even a foot—to have had your story, in your words, or the words of a female contemporary, to light the way.

Adrienne Rich said, "We must use what we have to invent what we desire."[19] What I desire is a world in which the you I have imagined could have existed, a world in which you lived your life with grace and agency.

---

18 Before the Christian conversion in the seventh century, there is no evidence that sexuality was a moral issue: no material culture, no text, nothing. For a detailed examination of the available information, see my research blog, *Gemæcce*. For more personal thoughts on Hild's sexuality, see my personal blog.

19 Adrienne Rich, *What Is Found There: Notebooks on Poetry and Politics* (W.W. Norton, 1993), 215.

History is our interpretation of what happened, our shared understanding of past events in the light of what we know today. I'm tired of the master story, his story. I'm tired of our story, my story, being a mystery. Tired of women never leading their people, tired of women never being heroic just because they can, of never changing the world because they want to. I'm so very tired of reading about women who get where they do by marrying into power or giving birth to those who will inherit it, of women who are more object than subject.

By writing your story I am looking at where we come from—the past—and believing we could have survived there as ourselves. By imagining you as possible, I am recasting what today we think might have *been* possible. By reclaiming the past, retelling it to include women as people, I'm remaking the present, and, I hope, changing the future.

In my version of the world, you are no longer missing.

The Women You Didn't See: A Letter to Alice Sheldon

Dear Alice,

You were brilliant, I think, but consumed by the inevitability of the abattoir. In your fiction all the gates are closed; characters are funnelled down a chute to flashing knives. In your best fiction, the characters know what is happening but the knowledge makes no difference; there's no way out.

You didn't believe in the possibility of escape. Assuming the persona of *James Tiptree Jr.* meant at least you could step outside the chute and be the one wielding the knife. *Raccoona Sheldon*, on the other hand, bound you—and us—inside the doomed and running cows; then you sometimes tantalised your victims with a vision of a better reality before tearing it to shreds before our eyes ("Your Faces, O My Sisters! Your Faces Filled of Light!"[1]), and sometimes you focused unwaveringly on the stark machinery of death ("The Screwfly Solution").[2] But for you there was no way out.

1 Raccoona Sheldon, "Your Faces, O My Sisters! Your Faces Filled of Light!" *Aurora: Beyond Equality* (Fawcett, 1976).

2 Raccoona Sheldon, "The Screwfly Solution," *Analog Science Fiction/ Science Fact 97*, no. 6 (June 1977): 54–57, 61–70, 72–73.

When you were little, you saw filth, death, deprivation, and suffering in India and Africa. So too, of course, did many of the hundreds of millions who lived there. Unlike many you were not, as far as I know, physically brutalised. But you were alone: a pretty, pampered, privileged little girl plunged unprepared into violent contradiction—then exposed by your writer mother just before puberty to the hot breath of public scrutiny. You had no herd protection, no people just like you, nowhere to turn for comfort or to take shelter. Did it warp you in the chrysalis? Or were you exactly as you were born to be?

We'll never know. It doesn't matter. But this, if I had to guess, is why you hid all your life. This is why you picked up professions and dropped them as soon as you got good, and why, when you found writing as an adult, you took pseudonyms: the best way to stay safe was to not be known. You could rotate a facet of yourself before a curtain with a single slit. No one ever got to see the whole, not even you.

We never met in person. I didn't smell your skin or feel the vibration of your voice. I can't call up a memory of how you moved or the way you responded to particular sounds. But I heard your written voice: I read your fiction. Now that you're beyond hurt, I admit: I did not admire your novels or your later short fiction. For this reader, you produced your best work when you were behind the curtain.

#

One of the things we don't know about that person who hid is whether choosing to write as a man meant you also wanted to be, or felt as though you were, a man.

You wrote a letter in response to Joanna Russ in which you

said, "I am a Lesbian."[3] If this is true, you identified as a woman who loved women—or tried—rather than as a man in the wrong body. Weighed against this is the youthful (I think, and, according to your biographer, probably drunken) *cri de coeur* scribbled in a sketch pad. "[I long to] ram myself into a crazy soft woman and come, come, spend, come, make her pregnant Jesus to be a man . . . I love women I will never be happy."[4] Given the (possible) youth and (probable) drinking this might be the melodrama of immaturity. It could be a test, an exploration of the kind teenagers indulge in, donning and doffing identities and attitudes to see what suits the emerging self. You emerged many times, of course, most spectacularly in middle age.[5] I suspect that if wanting to be a man was a thing of the body rather than the spirit, if you wanted physically to have been born a man—as opposed to yearning to be treated with the respect usually reserved to men—being among women would not have made you feel free or proud. But

---

3 A letter Sheldon sent to Russ. "Oh, had 65 years been different! I like some men a lot, but from the start, before I knew anything, it was always girls and women who lit me up." From a review of the Phillips (below) by Elizabeth Hand: https://www.sfsite.com/fsf/2006/eh0610.htm, (accessed April 30, 2015). This direct quote from Sheldon, and others below, are from Julie Phillips, *James Tiptree, Jr.: The Double Life of Alice B. Sheldon* (St. Martin's, 2006).

4 https://www.sfsite.com/fsf/2006/eh0610.htm (accessed April 30, 2015).

5 "How many times in one's life does a door open to total escape, utter newness? I was so profoundly dispirited, alienated [. . .] And suddenly I was in the middle of a different light, a new me, first having a good joke of being someone else, and then as the stories went on and out, having started genuine friendships among delightful people whose native language—crude, childish, humorous—rational—was mine . . ." http://jamestiptreejr.com/asawriter.htm (accessed April 30, 2015).

that's exactly how you felt when you joined the Women's Army Corps: "first time I ever felt free enough to be proud."[6]

We don't know, we can't know. So I will take you at your word: you were a lesbian, a woman who loved women.

#

There are two words—both with the same root in *covert*, the past participle of *covrir*, Old French for to cover—that I suspect you understood in your bones: covert and coverture. I have no doubt that as part of the CIA you were deeply and consciously familiar with the denotation, connotations and consequence of the former. The latter is a legal doctrine, probably introduced to English common law by the Normans, by which a wife's legal identity is covered and subsumed by her husband's. As Wikipedia puts it, in a marriage there is only one person, and that person is the husband. Some aspects of coverture survived into the second half of the twentieth century—more than fifty years after you were born.

This doctrine influenced the relative status, behaviour, and regard (including self-regard) of women and men. Men were real people, judged as such. Women were not. And it's my belief that "James Tiptree Jr.," three words, gave you cover, a way to be free

---

6 ". . . in the rain, under the flag, the sound of the band, far-off, close, then away again; the immortal fanny of our guide, leading on the right, moved and moving to the music—the flag again—first time I ever felt free enough to be proud of it; the band, our band, playing reveille that morning, with me on KP since 0430 hours, coming to the mess-hall porch to see it pass in the cold streets, under that flaming middle-western dawn; KP itself, and the conviction that one is going to die; the wild ducks flying over that day going to PT after a fifteen-mile drill, and me so moved I saluted them [. . .]" http://jamestiptreejr.com/army.htm (accessed April 30, 2015).

in the world without risking a particular scrutiny. A man, even a clearly pseudonymous one, is judged as a person and not for the myriad ways she is a not-quite-person. Given your experience, you believed Tiptree could be a writer. Alice Sheldon could only have been a female not-quite-person who wrote.

It's likely, then, that you became Tiptree because as a man you could write what you think and how you feel, be respected and liked. You deserved to live in a place of respect, a place we all deserve, a place we all belong: recognised as real people without having constantly to fight to be a human being.

So why did you—ex-CIA—let slip a vital piece of information about the death of your mother? Did you want, on some level, to be revealed? Or did grief fuck with your head? Grief does that.

Whatever the reason, you were grieving far more than your mother when your first novel came out under the Tiptree byline but was understood to be written by Alice Sheldon. You were mourning the cover and camouflage that kept you secret, kept you safe. You had lost the hidden place that felt like home. Once again, you were exposed to the world.

#

I'm a woman. A dyke. Foreign (even in the UK, where now I'm often thought to be Canadian). A cripple. In today's parlance I suffer a lot of intersectional microaggression: the constant, mostly unintentional but damaging nonetheless, insult of unthinking words and attitudes scraping along my hull below the waterline. Most of us in oppressed groups tend to seek out our own kind as a matter of survival; people like us offer us a mirror, a place to belong and be understood. Shelter from the cold.

I'm the only English expat lesbian cripple I know. It gets lonely.

Being out my whole life—even when I was four I knew I would not marry a man; actually falling in love with a woman when I was fifteen was just a detail—meant I had nowhere to hide. Queer was the only minority I knew without grants, government departments or liaisons, laws, schools, or families of origin who understood how hard it is, and whose mission was your encouragement and support. I felt isolated, alone. I've no doubt you did, too. Many of us do.

So I understand why you might not have wanted to be out in the early twentieth century. Being out was hard. It cost a lot.

#

Of your major works, "The Women Men Don't See" is singular. The two women our traveller meets don't know what they're heading towards, exactly, whether they are jumping from the frying pan into the fire. They know only that they are burning and must leap.

Two things about this story interest me particularly. First, we are left with hope for the women. It's only a sliver, true, and sharp with irony, but it's there. Second, neither of the women has—as far as we know—suffered physical violence. They are damaged, yes—as are all of us who, day in and day out, navigate cold and hostile waters, scraped and battered and weighed down by that ice—but not broken, not essentially breached. They will live. They are making a choice.

It's a forced choice, but a choice. We are shown some of their circumstances but not all; we have to make assumptions. We can't know for sure whether what they're doing is a good idea. Similarly, we can never know a writer's reasons. We can make assumptions—about why, say, for one woman gender-neutral initials will be enough to provide cover to write; why another keeps an obviously female name but clears her path by hosing everything with rage; why yet a third takes a male name—but we can never know. They all grow in different microclimates, under different gravities.

Living under a higher gravity than those around us levies a weight penalty: we have to use more energy, more strength, more attention to run the same distance and hurdle the same obstacles.

#

I listened the other day to a panel of women talk about diversity in fiction. They talked about how difficult it was to grow up as immigrants to another culture, how they were pressured by family to succeed in a profession—engineering, medicine, law—rather than art. I resonated with some of their experience but in another way I could not. I could not imagine growing up in a world where my family and wider society assumed I was capable of a profession, where I would be welcome in a profession, where I could survive in a profession.

I can't know anyone's struggles. I do know that they and you and I laboured under different burdens; our eras, places, classes, and cultures were different. But for the women on that panel access to a profession was a given. We may as well have been born on different planets.[7]

#

---

7 This makes me glad—though every now and again my gladness is bittersweet. This is something anyone from any traditionally downtrodden minority understands: the new generation has no clue how hard it was. We are happy for that. Mostly. And we worry they might not have our hard-earned skills to survive the inevitable backlashes.

Today, women and quiltbag folk still live under a greater gravity than others but that is changing every day. Hopefully, by the time others read this the gravity will have dropped a notch: same-sex marriage will be the law of the land. I've written elsewhere about how, in my opinion, this will begin to change gender equality on a fundamental level.[8] It will take time, of course; it always does. There will be steps back; there always are. But what I'm getting at is that already, today, there are women growing up who will not labour under any weight penalty.

Girls losing their milk teeth today will become women who won't have the faintest idea what coverture means unless they become historians. These women will be able to put their strength, attention, and brilliance into forging new paths, making new connections, dreaming of new possibilities rather than carrying extra weight or keeping themselves safe.

These are the women you didn't see. They will own the world.

---

8 "Wife," June 23, 2014, https://nicolagriffith.com/2014/06/23/wife/ (accessed April 30, 2015); also included in this volume.

Iceberg

It's hard to think
with nine-tenths of your heart
below the surface
Hard to talk
when what remains
glints in the light
flinging shards of sun
to leave friends blinded and afraid

Crippled Body

Wrecked
wrack washed up
etched and salted
drying to crystal glitter:
wrack
not ruin

Love-Hate

hate set me running
            like a thin black dog
with hard-cleat boots
at you

hate hit my bloodstream
            in a thick red flood
that will burn the skin
off you

hate kept me grinding
up that long brown hill
where I jumped
full hard
on you

Thief

(after Anonymous, 8th C)

You have taken the laugh from me
You have taken the light from me
You have taken the dawn
 and the night
You have taken before from me
You have taken the after
 the warp and the weft
You have taken the best

What is left?
You have taken the answer

Glimmer

THEY SAID IT MIGHT hurt—and it might, but not yet. Though yet has no meaning; yet is as empty as a gourd. But because they said it might hurt she ate nothing, before (after? soon? never?) so she, too, is empty. Empty, yet now she begins to fill a line between one galaxy and the next, to slide into the otherwhere like a drug being pushed through the skin of reality and delivered from one state to another.

Something is happening. She is pulsing, lengthening, cooling, a cord stretched past the horizon along which she slides like a bead. She feels like loam and light.

Some arrive younger, some arrive older. She would like to arrive without the holes burned through the myelin sheathing her spinal cord; she would like to walk again. She might arrive with no spinal cord, or during her last breath. It is a risk, they tell her before she signs her agreement in DNA. But she imagines a moment of arrival, pouring back into herself and blinking, opening her eyes to a new sky with new stars over a new city. She takes a breath, and her lungs feel clean and elastic, and she sits up with an ease she has not had since she was twenty. She looks at the back of her hands: she is twenty. The skin is like a child's: dewy, unmarked, springy as the moss she loved to lie on to look at the clouds. She laughs and leaps up—

But she is still pouring from one cup of universe to another, and now she is glimmering. To glimmer is to feel an endless Brownian motion in the soul—a transport phenomenon. The exchange of mass, energy, charge, and angular momentum between observed and studied systems. But she is not observed. She doesn't know where she is; no one knows. Where does the light go when you turn it off? She could be arcing across the universe like a howl, or a slice of light, or the scent of lemon, or she could still be lying down on that cold, corrugated platform.

When she got in, naked—No tooth implants? No lens replacements? Interior mesh, heart valve, titanium joint? Nail or hair extensions? No, she said. Good, they said, because it can get . . . messy—and lay down, it hurt, like lying on pebbles or an upside-down sunbed, lying on the lid of tubes instead of the padding.

No, this is wrong, she wanted to say. No, she's changed her mind. No, stop. But perhaps they were used to that, perhaps they had drugs, because now a great lassitude filled her and between forming the thought and opening her mouth, aeons passed and galaxies turned, and the impulse evaporated. There was no countdown, no last-minute reassurance. There were no longer minutes. No body, no mind. Perhaps she evaporated and was blown away by a breath.

The universe, the multiverse is vast, endless, infinite and she is empty, but she expands to fill it, drifting in the cosmic wind.

And now she begins to eddy, to gather and condense. She is gathering to a point, and falling, and now there is sound: a cathedral drip, becoming a harmonic echo which turns into a hum, a rush, a cataract. Yet still she is pouring from one state to another, still evaporating from herself, still being pushed through the skin of reality, still plunging into forever-never-other, to elsewhere. She is in simultaneous states of phase: everywhere, nowhere, nothing.

But with the sound she begins to feel weight. How much does change weigh? How much does time weigh? How much does hope weigh?

Hope is a heavy burden. It can stop you trying what you need. If you hope you will one day walk again, you will try drugs, you will try muscle stimulation, you will try exoskeletons that reek of silicone lubricant and dread. You will not try the wheelchair until your heart is shrivelled by fear and failure; you will discover the ease of gliding motion too late to prevent the de/formation of a hard, protective shell which did not protect you, did not keep out the lapping rise of despair and self-hatred.

Why me? she had asked. What do you want with a cripple for your far and fabulous colony? You are rare and precious, they said. Your genes are one in ten million: they are the key that unlocks the gate. We can send you and you'll get there, and you'll get there while you're still alive. We don't know how long you'll live, we can't make sense of that part yet, but with your genes you'll be alive, and apart from MS you're healthy. You're bright—

She's bright and plays well with others, her reports said. Mostly. She plays well with others when she gets her own way, which is a lot. She was a golden child, full of promise. A golden adult, glowing and graceful, until the holes began to etch themselves on her spine and the signal to her legs faltered and the nerve impulse sputtered and went out.

But she could arrive before the disease began, before the legion of lesions. Oh let that happen and she will never smoke she will never drink she will never eat carbs or saturated fat or dairy or sugar. She will always get her sleep, will exercise regularly, and always always play nicely, if only she may have her way in this one thing.

How much does hope weigh? It is too heavy. It is slowing her down. And now the sound is a roar, the roar of braking, and now she can smell burning. She is burning, her blood is burning.

Think.

What is fire? Heat and light and excitation. She will keep the heat of joy, the light of thought, the excitement of the new, but she will not burn. She will not.

She will flow in a steady glimmering stream from one reality to another. She will fill slowly with herself until she is right here, right now, and ready to face what will come. She is here. She has arrived.

Cold Wind

From the park on Puget Sound I watched the sun go down on the shortest day of the year. The air lost its lemon glitter, the dancing water dulled to a greasy heave, and the moon, not yet at its height, grew more substantial. Clouds gathered along the horizon, dirty yellow-white and gory at one end, like a broken arctic fox. Snow wasn't in the forecast, but I could smell it.

More than snow. If all the clues I'd put together over the years were right, it would happen tonight.

I let the weather herd me from the waterfront park into the city, south then east, through the restaurant district and downtown. The streets should have been thronged with last-minute holiday shoppers but the weather had driven them towards the safety of home.

By the time I reached the urban neighbourhood of Capitol Hill, the moon was behind an iron lid of cloud, and sleet streaked the dark with pearl.

Inside the women's bar, customers were dressed a little better than usual: wool rather than fleece, cashmere blend instead of merino, and all in richer, more celebratory colours. The air was spiced with cinnamon and anticipation. Women looked up when the door opened, they leaned towards one another, faces alight like children waiting for their teacher to announce a story, a present, a visit from Santa.

The holidays, time out of time. Mørketiden or Mōdraniht, Solstice or Soyal, Yaldā or Yule or the Cold Moon Dance, it doesn't matter what people call the turn of the year; it fills them with the drumbeat of expectancy. Even in cities a mammalian body can't escape the deep rhythms imposed by the solar cycle and reinforced by myth. Night would end. Light would come.

Daylight. Daybreak. Crack of dawn. You can tell a lot about a culture from its metaphors: the world is fragile, breakable, spillable as an egg. People felt it. Beyond the warmth and light cast by the holiday they sensed predators roaming the dark. It made people long to be with their own kind. Even those who were not usually lonely hungered to belong.

I sat by the window, facing the door, and sipped Guinness black as liquorice and topped with a head like beige meringue. I savoured the thrust of rusty-fist body through the velvet glove of foam, glad of the low alcohol. Daybreak was a long way off.

Three women in front of me were complaining about babysitters; someone's youngest had chicken pox and another urged her to throw a holiday pox party so they could get all their children infected at once. After all, wasn't it better for the body to get its immunity naturally, the old-fashioned way?

It was one of the most pernicious fallacies, common the world over: Old ways are best. But old ways can outlast their usefulness. Old ways can live on pointlessly in worlds that have no room for them.

I drained my beer and almost, from force of habit, recorded my interaction with the server when she took my order for a refill. But I wasn't here to work and, besides, it would have given me nothing useful, no information on the meeting of equals: the customer is always a little higher on the food chain, at least on the surface.

A woman in the far corner was smiling at me. A woman with the weathered look of a practiced alcoholic. I smiled back; it was the holidays. She brightened. If I brightened in turn she would wave me over. "Let's not be alone at Christmas," she'd say. And I could say . . . anything. It wouldn't matter because drunks forget it all before they reach the bottom of the glass. I could say: I'm so very, very tired of being alone. I ache, I yearn, I hunger for more.

But women like her would never be my more. So I shook my head and raised my glass with the inclination of the head that, the world over, meant: *Thank you. We are done.*

I sipped my Guinness again, looked at the sky—the sleet was getting whiter—and checked the time. Not yet. So I tuned them all out and listened to the music, a heartfelt rendition of an old blues piece by a woman with a clearly detectable English accent beneath the Delta tones. The music, at least, did not make me feel like an outsider. It was an old friend. I let it talk to me, let it in, let the fat, untuned bass drum, timed to a slow heartbeat, drive the melody into the marrow of my long bones where it hummed like a bee, and the river of music push against the wall of my belly . . .

. . . and they were speaking Korean at a table against the wall, which took me back to the biting cold of the Korean DMZ, the mud on the drinking hole sprinkled with frost, the water buffalo and her calf—

The door slammed open bringing with it a gust of snowy air—and a scent older than anything in the city. Every cell in my body leapt.

Two women came in laughing. The one in jeans and a down vest seemed taller, though she wasn't. Her cheeks were hectic, brown eyes brilliant, and not only from the cold. Women have lit up that way for thousands of years when they have found someone they want, someone whose belly will lie on theirs heavy and soft and urgent, whose weight they welcome, whose voice thrills them, whose taste, scent, turn of the head makes them thrum with need, ring and sing with it. They laugh. They glow.

The other was paler, her eyes brown, too, wide set. Deep brown, velvet. Snow dappled her hair. She stood by the door, blinking, as people do when they walk from dark into light.

My aorta opened wide and blood gushed through every artery, all my senses gearing up. But I pretended not to see her. I gazed out of the window, at the sleet turning to snow, the air clotting with cold, and the pavement softening from black to grey. Reflected in the glass the women around me were coming alert, spines straightening, cheeks blooming, capillaries opening.

She was here. She was real. I'd been right.

The woman in the down vest smiled, touched the other on the shoulder, and said something. They moved through the doorway to the pool room and out of sight.

I'd been right. I relished the realisation because soon I wouldn't be able to; soon my mind would be submerged and I'd be lost in a pull almost as old as the turning of the seasons. I watched the snow come down in streetlight cold as moonlight and, for a moment, missed the old sodium lamps with their warm yellow glow, their hint of hearth and home and belonging.

I pondered her clothes: long dress, with a thick drape; long coat of oddly indeterminate colour; boots. Those were long, too. Not shiny. Brown? Black? I frowned. I couldn't tell. It didn't matter. She was here. It would go as it would.

I moved into energy-conservation mode, as in the field when watching groups whose habits you know as well as your own name: reflexes begun but arrested, peripheral vision engaged. Around me the bar moved from hot to simmering and now a new scent undercut the usual wood-and-hops of microbrews and the holiday cinnamon: the sting of liquor. Someone turned up the music. Two women at different tables—one of the Koreans and a gap-toothed white girl—exchanged glances; one followed the other to the bathroom.

The snow fell steadily. Traffic would be snarling the intersections, blocked by buses slid sideways down the hill. Soon those vehicles would be abandoned and the streets utterly empty. The CCTV would be locked with cold.

Soon.

The foam on the inside of my glass sagged like a curtain swag then slid to the bottom. I'd drunk it faster than I'd meant. At the table by the wall a Korean voice was raised—her girlfriend had taken too long in the bathroom, "Because there are two crazy women in there!"

The bathroom.

But as I stood the world swam and lost focus for a moment, then reformed around the doorway from the pool room. She stepped through. Her long coat was fastened to the collar. Toggled with horn, not buttoned. It looked beige and cream against the doorjamb but grey-blue in its shadowed folds. Perfect camouflage.

She saw me. Her face didn't move, but I knew how it would be when she flung her head back, cried out, clutched my shoulders as she shuddered. I felt her breath against my collarbone as she folded there, the brush of her mouth against my skin.

She came towards me, stepping around the spilt beer and dropped fries, lifting her feet high, placing them carefully, as though she wore tall heels.

I watched, unable—unwilling—to move.

And then she stood before me. I could smell her—woodland, fern, musk—and I wanted to reach, fold her down, stretch her out on the bracken, and feel the pulse flutter at her neck.

"You were watching me," she said, and her voice sounded hoarse, as though used to a bigger throat.

"I'm . . . an anthropologist. It's what we do." I've been looking for you for a long time. I didn't think you existed.

"What's your name?"

I thought about that. "Onca."

She nodded; it meant nothing to her. Her eyes were so dark. She turned up her collar. "I'll see you, Onca. Soon, I hope." A cold stream purled through her voice and snow blew across her eyes. *Come outside, under the sky with me*, they said.

I nodded. We both knew I would: She called, others followed. It's who she was.

And then she was gone. I didn't look out of the window. If the stories were true in this way too, I wouldn't be able to see her, not yet.

#

I found her victim in the bathroom, the blind spot with no cameras. She wasn't dead. She sat propped on the seat in a stall, jeans around her knees, head against the wall.

She grinned at me foolishly. "Can't move."

I locked the stall behind me. "Does it hurt?"

"Naw."

It would. I smelled blood, just a little. I bent, looked at her shirt darkening between her breasts. "Can you draw a deep breath?"

She tried. In reality it was more of a sigh. But she didn't flinch or cough. No broken ribs.

I squatted in front of her, elbows on knees, hands dangling comfortably. She just kept smiling, head at that odd angle against the wall. In that position she couldn't see me. I stood, straightened her head, then, because it was distracting, I leaned her on my shoulder, lifted, and pulled up her jeans. She could fasten them herself later, or not.

I squatted again, regarded her. She was still smiling, but it was a faint echo of what it had been. No longer solid. After this not much would be. "There's a legend," I said. "More than a dozen legends, from all over the world." La Llorona. Or Flura. Xana, Iara, Naag Kanya . . . "She lures people with sex. Some say she takes your heart." Sometimes literally. "But she always takes something." I considered her. "She's taken your spirit."

"My . . ."

I waited, but she didn't say any more. "Your soul." As good a word as any. "You're tired, I should think."

Her smile faded, like a guttering flame. She might survive. She would never feel alive again.

I wasn't sure she could hear me anymore. I leaned forwards, unbuttoned her shirt. The bruise was swelling too quickly to be sure, but the shape cut into the broken skin—lovely skin, over firm muscle—could have been from a blow by a hoof.

"What's your name?"

"María José Flores."

"María, you make me hungry." And she would have, with her spirit intact. "But not like this." I fastened her back up and stood. Time to go.

#

The city was another world in the snow. Silent. Flakes falling soft as owl feathers. Time out of time.

The streets were empty. No traffic in or out. It would last until she was done. I'd traced her through campfire stories, elders' tales, academic papers, psychiatric reports; it's what she did. She had been new in the world when the conquistadores came; alone. Over the centuries she had refined her methods until they were ritual: she fed early on the evening of a winter high day or holiday, brought her strength to peak, then chose someone to play with all night. Someone strong. Someone who would last.

I had put myself in her path and she had chosen me, and now I must seek her out. But as I did, as I followed her, she was shadowing me, herding me. I didn't try to pinpoint her—she was at the height of her powers, luxuriant with María Flores—but I knew she was there somewhere, behind the abandoned, snow-shrouded cars, in the doorway, behind the dumpster and the frozen cameras. I felt her on my left, a presence as subtle as atmospheric pressure, turning me north. I knew where she wanted me to go. So I padded through the muffled white dream downtown had become, pacing my shadow along the old brick and concrete walls of back streets and alleys, towards the edge of the city, where land met sea.

Alleys widened to open space and the sky glimmered with reflected water light. The land began to climb and undulate. Under the snow, pavement softened to grass and then alternating gravel path and turf on dirt layered on concrete. A switchback over a road. The sculpture park overlooking the Sound.

Before I reached the brow of the hill I stopped and listened. Silence. So profound I heard the snow falling, settling with a crystalline hiss, bright and sharp as stars. I closed my eyes, opened my mouth a little, breathed and tongued the air to the roof of my mouth. There. To the west. Where there should be only the cold snow, industrial solvents beneath the thin layer of topsoil trucked in and grassed over, and the restless damp of the Sound. The sharp tang of woman, of beast.

I opened my eyes, let blood flood the muscles of my shoulders and thighs, and listened.

The snow stopped. A breath of wind ruffled my hair. The clouds thinned from iron to mother-of-pearl, lit from above by moonlight. To the west, the Sound shimmered.

Eyes unfocused, vision wide to catch motion, I saw the shadow picking its way over the snow. If I closed my eyes I would hear the lift and delicate step of a doe moving through undergrowth.

I moved again, keeping low, east then south. I stopped. Coughed, deliberately, and felt as much as heard her ears flick and nostrils flare as she tracked my position. Come, I thought, come to me.

And she did. She crossed the skyline and I saw her clearly.

Her coat was winter beige, thick and soft, pale as underfur at her throat and where it folded back as she walked. Her knees bent the wrong way. Her dark boots were not boots.

Deer Woman.

I took off my jacket and dropped it in the snow. I opened my shirt.

She stopped, nostrils opening and closing. Her head moved back, her right leg lifted as though to stamp. But there was no herd to signal. She kept coming.

She wanted me to run, so I did. I bounded away, moving through trees—they were not big enough to climb—north and east, leaping the concrete wall, loping between the looming sculptures, until I was among the cluster of greenery at the corner of the park. She followed.

Two hundred years ago, even a hundred, when there were still wolves in the north of this country and big cats in the south, she would have been more careful, but she had been playing predator, not prey, for too long. No doubt she had lost count of nights like this, the victims whose fear for a while overwhelmed their attraction. She would take her time, not risk her legs on those walls. She was still sleek with María, and this was the height of her yearly rite, not to be rushed.

The sky was almost white now. Against it, bare twigs stood out like black lace. I couldn't see the water from here but I could smell it. It softened the air, utterly unlike the arid cold of Korea, coarse as salt. Korea, where it was rumoured that the Amur leopard was back in the DMZ.

The snow crunched. Closer, so much closer than I expected; I'd been careless, too. She was not a buffalo calf.

Moonlight spilled through the cloud and splashed onto the snow and I saw the darker line in the grey-blue shadow of the steel sculpture.

"Onca," it said. "Come to me."

Recklessness burst in me, brilliant as a star. I stood, and left the safety of the trees.

Moon shadow is steep and sharp. The tracks I made looked like craters. Her scent ripened, rich and round against the keen night air. I swallowed.

"I can't see you." My voice was ragged, my breath fast.

She stepped from the shadow.

I moved closer. Closer still, until I could see the pulsing ribbon of artery along her neck, the snowflake on a thread of her hair. Strong hair, brown-black.

"Kneel," she said. She wanted me beneath her in the snow. She would fold down on me and crush the breath from my lungs until my heart stopped and she could lap me up and run, run through the trees, safe, strong for another year.

"No," I said.

She went very still. I regarded her. After a moment I stepped to one side so she could see my tracks.

She took a step backward. It wouldn't be enough. It would never have been enough, even in the long ago.

"Who are you?"

"Onca." My newest name, *Panthera onca*. "B'alam before that. And long, long ago, Viima." She didn't understand. I'd been a myth before she was born.

I waited.

She looked at the tracks again: a half-moon and four circles. Unmistakable.

She shot away, all deer now, straight for the trees lining Western Avenue. They always go for the trees.

In the DMZ the water buffalo had been heavier, and horned, but only a buffalo, nothing like my equal. Deer Woman ran like a rumour, like the wind, but I was made for this, and though I hadn't hunted one of my kind for an age, had thought I had taken the last a lifetime ago, she had never run from one like me. I was older. Much older. And at short range, cats are faster than deer.

I brought her down with one swipe to the legs and she tumbled into the snow. She panted, tail flickering. Her hind legs tightened as she prepared to scramble up and run again. I stood over her. I could take her throat in my jaws and suffocate her until she was a heartbeat from death, then rip her open and swallow her heart as it struggled to beat, feel its muscular contraction inside me. The lungs next. Rich with blood. Slippery and dense. Then the shoulders.

But she didn't move, and I didn't move, and she was a woman again.

"Why?" Her hoarse voice seemed more human now. She didn't know why she was still alive.

I didn't, either. "Cold Wind. That was my first name, before there was a land bridge, and long before the land bridge drowned. You think you're old . . ."

I looked at the steel sculpture: huge, undeniable, but rust would eat it as surely as leaves fall in winter and dawn breaks the night open, and I would still be here. Alone. I had killed them all, because that was what I did.

"Get up," I said.

"Why?"

"So you can run."

Surely she wasn't weary of life, not yet, but she began to lift her jaw, to offer her throat. Cats are faster than deer. I would catch her, and as young as she was, she felt it: This was who we were, this was what we did. It was the old way.

"Run. I won't kill you. Not this year."

Silence. "But next?"

Predator and prey. We were the last. I said nothing. And she was gone, running, running.

The stars shone bright but the moon was setting and more cloud was on its way, ordinary northwest cloud. The night was warming, the silence already thinning, traffic starting up again at the edges. By tomorrow the snow would melt, the cameras would work. But tonight it was still a cold world where Deer Woman ran towards daybreak, and I had someone to hunger for.

Down the Path of the Sun

I DREAMED AGAIN: MY sister Diggy and I were on the beach. Although we were the same age as we are now, it was before the plague: my father and three other sisters were there, too, shadowy and indistinct. Like ghosts. We sat facing each other on the sand, surrounded by a bubble of quiet, digging.

Something got tossed ashore on a breaker: a shell, the colour of caramel and milk, big as my fist and smooth as ivory. I wanted it, even though it was forbidden.

Diggy breathed at my shoulder. I reached out and took the shell.

The air rolled and the sea heaved, sluggish as soup; Diggy's eyes widened in fear. I should have uncurled my fingers, let the shell drop onto the sand; given in. Instead, I gripped it tighter; I had found some infinitely precious thing to enrich my life always.

The seagod came roaring out of the waves. The air trembled with his anger but only Diggy and I could see him. We began to run. Everyone began to run: the sea was gaining. We were not going to make it. Still, I refused to drop the shell.

A huge wave crashed down and I leapt for the railings topping the sea wall. I caught them, held them. I had won. Then, with sickening inevitability, I realised that I did not see Diggy anywhere.

She was clinging, half-submerged, to my right ankle. Above the crash and hiss of the spray I could hear her screaming: Karo! Help me!

The tidal wave fell on us.

There was nothing I could do. I lay against the wall, holding on with the strength of desolation while one hand, then the other, was torn from my ankles. I still had my shell, my infinitely precious shell, but Diggy was gone. The seagod had devoured her.

#

I woke on my back, heart thumping hard enough to break bones. I lay still, listening to the lap of water against stone down below.

Next to me, Fin twitched in her sleep, trying to pull back the blankets I must have dragged from us while I dreamed. Carefully, I slid off the opened-up sleeping bag and tucked her up. I kissed her but resisted the urge to stroke the hair straggling from her braid. Fin's hair is like Fin, wiry and black, always pulling free of restraint. She pulled me along, too; knowing Fin, I knew that grief was not everything, that Evelyn, my mother, was wrong.

I pulled on a shirt and loose trousers before I pushed past the curtain that partially divided the soaring height of the warehouse's fourth floor. Old Will lifted his head and banged his tail on the floorboards as I crossed to where he lay next to my little sister in the corner. With one hand I scrubbed at his head behind his ears, the other I held by Diggy's face. She breathed, warm and soft against my palm. My relief was immediate, as always. I squatted back on my heels and contented myself with watching her eyelids flutter as she lived through some dream of her own. The predawn light gleamed on the hair framing her girl-plump face: silver blond around lightly toasted gold. Since the plague, Diggy had become more and more my responsibility. I glanced over to where my mother slept and felt the familiar confusing mix of helplessness, love, and anger.

By the window, away from the warmth of sleeping bodies, the cold of an April dawn pushed easily through the thin cotton to my skin.

I rested my elbows on the sill and stared eastward to where other warehouses gaped open to the lightening sky; beyond them lay the sea. Eight years it had been like this: families like mine, like Fin's, finding and comforting each other in the quiet, in the emptiness that we would never fill. Since the plague, I had crossed paths with fewer than forty women and only a handful of men; all of us sterile.

#

It had rained in the night and the air was fresh with damp early summer greenness. Here and there tiny puddles winked in the sun. The sky was dotted with cloud, but the sun streamed from a wide patch of blue and my sweater lay warm across my shoulders. Fin could tell I did not want to talk and moved just ahead of me, gliding smooth and sure over the weed-patched cobbles. Now and then she disappeared, blending into shadow as she slipped, dart-slim, through a doorway or peered through a window cluttered with nature's rubbish.

Sometimes, when we walked like this along the dockfront, I tried to remember what it had all been like before, when there were thousands of well-fatted and loud-voiced people with Norfolk accents filling and emptying these warehouses all year round; when for every one who grew old and died, there was another new life to take their place. No one was well-fatted now, not the people like me and Evelyn, or Fin and her grandmother Jess. Not the gangs either, though they were loud voiced. Those gangwomen and men had the same strut and cruelty as Jess's little bantam rooster. Except the rooster made me laugh with his piercing eye and puffed-up chest. I had not seen a gang for three or four years. Luckily, they had not seen me. Jess reckoned they had probably all died—killed each other off and good riddance she said. But we still slept on the fourth floor and Fin still checked doorways and windows. We all carried knives, even Diggy, and Fin carried a garrotte as well. Old habits died hard.

#

The sun was a full arm span above the horizon now, the only sound birdsong and the wavelets slapping up onto the waterway's silted banks. We lay hip to hip and rib to rib in the middle of the wild wheat. The green ears flicked and rustled in the breeze.

We smiled, lazy after love. I ran my hand gently over the curve of Fin's hip, into the dip and over the upsweep of ribs and breast. Fillets of muscle slid beneath my hand. My skin, tanned though it was, looked pale as sap wood against the loamy darkness of hers. We rested like that a while.

The old waterway ran directly east where, with other waterways, it joined with the river mouth and the sea. The times that we had got here in time to watch the dawn, we noticed there was a slight tide which pulled eastward, to where the sun came up. The light seemed to suck the water towards it; I had seen twigs, even ducks, floating gently eastward to the sea. Fin called it the path of the sun.

We were too late for the sunrise today and, anyway, we were there for the eggs. We left our boots and trousers by the waterside and waded in opposite directions along the bank searching for egg-filled nests. Sometimes we would find none, sometimes so many that if we collected them all we would need to make two journeys with the basket. As I waded thigh deep, I knew this was going to be one of those unlucky days.

All around me the wheat clicked and rattled; the few clouds I had seen earlier now covered half the sky. The breeze was rising, sending cloud shadow racing over mile after mile of swaying gold and green. A long time ago, all this had been fen, wild and full of water creatures, until the farmers had dug their irrigation channels and planted their crops, draining the land of variety and vitality. Further inland, waterways were silting up leaving standing pools where weeds and rushes thrived, choking the wheat. The water birds and river creatures were coming back.

A cloud covered the sun and I shivered. I had found nothing and it was getting chilly. Time to go back.

Fin was already rubbing herself dry with her bandanna. Only two eggs, she said, not worth carrying back to Evelyn and Diggy. We cracked them and sucked, threw the empty shells away.

#

Fin's family had taken over a barn for the summer, half for them, half for their animals; above us, where we sat around the huge scarred table eating and talking, the roof looked to be more gap than tile. It was early evening. The sun poured through the chinks and the open door like old wine.

As Jess jabbed her fork in the air to emphasize a point, or stretched across the table to help herself to more salad, her knobby wrists flickered through hanging beams of light and shadow. Lean, with hair the grey of charcoal ash, she was the only one of the family who looked like Fin. Leoni and Sara, her daughters, looked to be just a little younger than Evelyn, and both were powerfully built women with pads of firm fat at hip and breast. Sara could look grim sometimes; she had a way of narrowing her eyes and pausing before she spoke. Leoni had a bad leg from a fall through a rotten floor two years ago. Between them they had three daughters: Fin, Rachael, and Else.

Evelyn called them a tribe, though they were not that many really; they had had their deaths just like anyone else. Maybe it was because they always talked and argued, made their decisions between them. In our family, the older you were, the more right you were. Inevitably, Evelyn was right all the time.

The muscles in my neck and shoulder tightened at the reminder that my mother always had to be right, like that time when I had come home with my hand in Fin's. She had known what it meant; Diggy had grinned.

"Diggy, leave the room."

"Let her stay, mother. We're a family."

She looked at Fin. "This isn't a family."

"It could be."

"This family died eight years ago."

"We can start again."

"No."

"Listen. Please. We could all live together, Fin's family and ours, sharing everything. We'd be safer, happier."

"Happier? You've never had children, Karo, you don't know what it's like to lose them and to know there'll never be any more."

"Do you want to lose me too?" I had asked, but quietly, so she would not hear.

#

Fin reached over and squeezed my hand. Tears dripped onto the scarred wood in front of me and someone handed me a strip of cloth to use as a handkerchief. No one spoke, but they understood: I had no real choices. I could not abandon Evelyn and Diggy and I could not change Evelyn's mind; she refused to understand.

The tears were stopping already. After a while we cleared the table and settled down to enjoy talk and stories in the last of the patchy sunshine.

#

Walking back from Fin's we trailed long shadows. The warehouse stood dark against the slow fire of the sky and suddenly, again, I was angry with Evelyn, a dull rage that ground at the base of my skull. Then we were clattering up the steps and my anger settled into its usual background crouch. I sighed, more concerned about Evelyn's disappointment when we came back without any eggs.

Halfway up the third flight, Fin flashed a smile over her shoulder. "Bread."

Then I smelled it too. Despite myself I felt a rare flush of affection for my mother: she knew there was nothing we liked better than fresh-baked bread. We slowed down, taking the steps one at a time, prolonging the anticipation.

The hot smell reminded me of when I was little, years before the plague: Evelyn, standing in a gleaming geometric kitchen, smartly shod feet on polished tile, kneading dough, sometimes letting me punch at it, sometimes disappearing through the door for a moment to make sure Diggy still slept. But always moving. Even when she relaxed, took off her apron and made coffee, her fingers would stray to the nape of her neck where she teased her permed hair back into its curls. That was a habit she still had, even though she often looked surprised when her fingers encountered hair absolutely straight from years away from the hairdresser. There was no apron now, no coffee or gleaming kitchen; while the bread baked in an old iron stove she had no toddler to amuse or baby to check on. Sometimes I had seen her sitting there blankly, almost like she had been turned off. It frightened me that she could look so empty. There was nothing wrong with daydreaming but with Evelyn it was different. Once, when I was ill and she thought I was asleep, she had sat like that for hours. When she had finally moved, she had looked about her incredulously, then shrugged. Ever since then, I had never been able to shake the feeling that my mother really did not believe that all this was real. The long-gone world of families and technology lived in her memories like yesterday. Maybe closer. She went about the business of life with an air of detachment, as though none of it really mattered.

#

For all its height and space, the fourth floor was hot. The last of the sun had poured directly in, mixing with the heat of bread steam and stove iron. Ignoring Evelyn's disapproval I propped the door open wide and stripped down to my shirt. Fin and I split one of the flat loaves and spent the next few minutes alternately tossing hot bread from hand to hand and burning our mouths.

I looked around, turned to Evelyn. "Where's Diggy?"

"She's not been back."

"Since when? Since she went to the food warehouse?"

Evelyn nodded.

"But she left before midday." I chewed slowly on my bread, refusing to get worried. Nothing could happen. She had a knife and knew how to use it and, besides, no one had seen a gang for years. She was hurt maybe, in a fall like Leoni's? No. Old Will would have come back here on his own. She could not be lost, she knew her way around as well as I did and, again, Will could have found his way home. No. She must be playing one of her child-woman games. I could just imagine her, warm and snug in the warehouse paper stacks, humming happily to herself, Will half asleep across her legs, totally oblivious to the worry she might be causing. She had done it before, more than once.

Without a word I began pulling sweater and trousers back on.

"I'll come with you," Fin said.

"No," I jerked my knife belt through the buckle. "Stay. Please. One of us may as well enjoy the bread while it's hot."

She looked at me steadily, then nodded: she would stay behind in case . . . in case anything happened that Evelyn would not be able to cope with.

Then I was down the steps and outside. The crunch of boot on stone seemed loud in the gathering dark. I trotted, then ran, trotted then ran, alternating between worry and irritation. The night was soft and warm; soon I was slick with sweat.

The warehouse I was heading for was a small one compared to most. Usually, we went in and out using a ground floor window but we had dragged open the great main doors just enough for Leoni and Evelyn to squeeze through. As soon as I saw those doors gaping wide I stopped. My body would not move a muscle; I was not even sure I was breathing. Was Diggy in there? Was anyone else? Without conscious direction, my body unfroze and lowered itself gently onto the cobbles. I cursed the moon; tonight it was no bigger than a nail clipping and its light only emphasized the shadow thrown by the doors. I lay there for a while, making no more noise than a spider weaving her web. I felt cold. Not the cold of the hard cobbles pushing bruises into my hips but a bleak numbness. Something had happened to stop me feeling anything except a kind of lightness in my long muscles. I listened a while longer then stood up, sheathed my knife and walked in.

It was the smell I would always remember: blood and shit. The air was thick with it, sweet and metallic. I spat into the dust and mud inside the door, trying to clear the taste from my mouth. I waited for moment to let unfamiliar shapes of shadow and moonlight come clearer. Several crates and sacks had been torn open, the contents scattered, destroyed. For one whirling moment, feeling threatened to return and overwhelm my false calm. I forced it away.

It was Old Will I saw first. His tail had been cut off and his back legs broken. By the blood trail and scuff marks, he had been able to drag himself quite a way before they had broken his back. Will, who had never known a blow or vicious word in his life. It was easy to imagine him running eagerly, as fast as his rheumatic legs would carry him, towards the gang who forced open the doors. How many had there been? Looking at the destruction, ten or more.

Methodically, I began to search for Diggy. Row by stacked row: I walked to the end then back again, slowly, checking behind this, on top of that. Then I began to shake. I tried to push it away again but it got worse, my legs would not hold me up. I knew where she was. I must have known from when I first set foot in the place because I had carefully avoided it. She would be in the paper stacks, or near there. Or what was left of her would be. The trembling stopped enough for me to stand up but I had to lean against a half-open sack of raw wool. It reeked, but not enough to cover the new smells, the sickening smells. Now that I thought I knew where she was my body seemed unwilling to obey me. For every step forwards I had to clench my jaws and fight the urge to run away, to run as far and as fast as I had ever run in my life.

Diggy had always liked to leave her legs bare, hating the restriction of trousers. Now they looked horribly, painfully naked. She was lying bent backwards over a roll of grey paper, her long shirt pulled up over her face and chest. One arm was trapped and tangled in the ripped and stained material, the other hung down, not quite touching the floor. Gently, I lifted her off the roll. She was heavier than usual and seemed to flop in all the wrong places. Before I laid her down, I straightened her shirt, buttoning it back up where it was not too badly torn. For a while I tried to get her broken leg to lie straight but then I gave up; it was already getting stiff. Teeth marks and bruises covered her body from the neck down, the rips and tears would not hide those. I was crying and the angry red marks and bloody smears kept splintering and merging then jumping back into focus as tears spattered my sweater. The feeling I had now was familiar: like after the dream. Except this was real, I would never again wake up to be reassured by her breathing.

By some chance that somehow made the other visible brutalities worse, Diggy's face was untouched. The tiny, gold-white wisps at her temples looked no different than they had this morning. There was a deep bruise on the back of her neck where they had broken it forcing her to arch over the roll. She stank, of their filth and her own blood and excreta. And there was a lot of blood. I would have to clean her up.

I soaked her shirt in water from outside and wiped at her carefully. I was dazed with hatred for those that had done this; hatred sang hot and light through my veins. I took off my own shirt and dressed her in it, hiding most of the ugliness. I looked for her missing sandal but could not find it. Very well. I took off her remaining one; that looked better. It was when I was combing through her hair with my fingers that I suddenly realised her neck sheath was empty. Where was her knife? My heart thumped like someone had kicked it. Where was Diggy's knife?

Then I was on my feet, feverishly pushing aside crates, plunging my hand into sacks. Where was her knife? I scraped my bare arms, bruised my spine shoving aside a rusted machine. I had to find the knife. If it was bloody then she had used it. That was important to me; I had to know. Where was that knife? I roared, trying to rattle the walls with the weight of my pain. I ran up and down the stacked aisles, desperate, frantic.

But it was not there. No knife. Tears were running steadily down my face now, splashing warm then turning cold on my bare chest. I knelt by Diggy's head and promised her she would have my knife, that I would put it in her sheath for her, that I would find her knife one day and use it for my own. And I cried until my face was swollen and my nose ran. Then I quieted and felt that strange lethargy you only get when you cannot cry any more.

That was how Fin found me, kneeling by Diggy's head, still and calm. She thought I was in shock but once she realised I was not, she knelt next to me in silence. After a little while I stirred and turned to her. We held each other and I wiped at her tears with my hand.

"They even killed the dog." Her voice was thick. "A dog. And poor Diggy."

I just nodded.

"I sent Evelyn to get Jess and the others."

"You sent her, and she went?"

"Yes."

There were no echoes in the warehouse. Every word hung dead in the air. I was trembling again.

Fin handed me my sweater. "Here, put it on." Of course, I was cold. I hardly noticed the irritation of wool on bare skin.

"Fin, her knife was gone. But I couldn't find it. Will you look? I've searched everywh—"

We froze at the tiny sounds from door and window. With a look of apology, Fin pulled my knife from Diggy's neck sheath and handed it to me. She slid her own out of leather and motioned for me to stay where I was.

"Fin! Karo! Are you in there?" Else's voice, strong but cautious.

"Diggy? Diggy? Are you there Diggy?" Evelyn, sounding weak and puzzled. I tried to answer but my throat had closed around my grief again. Rachael and Else padded feline and dangerous around the warehouse. I heard Fin explaining, Jess cursing, Evelyn shouting for Diggy again and again until Sara shut her up. The air was hot with adrenalin, we were all breathing very fast.

Jess stooped to help me up. She stood for a moment with her tree root hands on my shoulders, letting old pain acknowledge new. Then she sighed and stepped aside: there was more.

I looked at Evelyn.

"Karo? Where's Diggy?" She started towards me. "Who are these people, why are we here?" She looked about. "Where's your father?"

I took her hand. It was limp and warm. "Don't worry. I'm here. You don't have to do anything. Why don't you go with Sara for now? I'll join you later."

She nodded vaguely and allowed Sara to steer her gently towards the door. My mother had finally retreated into her land of yesterdays forever. Rachael and Else followed them out; Jess stayed. She looked down at Diggy.

"Where will you take her?"

"Out to sea."

She nodded, then looked straight at me. Her eyes were bright. "We'll take care of Evelyn for now. Tomorrow we'll talk for a long time."

#

We stood waist deep in the water, silent and waiting. In front of us, Diggy's floating bier of woven rushes was already tugging against our hands. The eastern sky was lightly touched with orange. This time yesterday I was feeling Diggy's breath on the back of my hand, laughing at my stupid dreams and noticing that her face was still plump with girl fat. It would never become lean and womanly. I would never know who Diggy would have become or might have chosen to love. And I would never know what had happened to her knife. So many things I would never know now.

Slowly, the water turned to fire; the tugging grew stronger. By my side, Fin looked serene; young and wise. Her hands were still and steady on the thick green stems. We had laid old Will on the front.

The bier tugged sharply. It was time. Without a word, we let it go and watched as it drifted eastward, down the path of the sun. Then I was humming a tune. Just a silly little thing. Diggy used to sing it to herself when she played. It was a catchy tune, easy to learn. Fin took it up for me when the melody was stifled by my tears, opening her throat to send Diggy on her way with a familiar song. As the bier drifted out of sight over the horizon, she raised both arms in salute. My infinitely precious Fin.

Close, but not touching, we walked back towards the barn and the other women; my family. All the way there we hummed that tune, Diggy's tune. The seagod had her now.

Many Things in Dumnet

LATE SUMMER, THE SKY a bright, hard blue, tiny white clouds turning to gold with the early evening sun. A gull wheeled and cried. And another. The ocean heaved, its surface brilliant, shading from almost-azure to the white-capped waves rolling in towards the crags and cliffs of Dumnet, most southwesterly of the kingdoms of Albion. The *Mermaid* was carrying Anya Reine into harbour.

Her brown hair, lightened almost to blond by sun and salt mist, was just long enough to be tied back with a strip of dark blue cloth which had been torn originally from the soft linen of her trousers. The skin around her eyes was tight. She looked older than she should. Today was her birthday. No one in the world knew this but herself, and Ude the theurgist. Ude, who was now an ocean away.

Today was also the anniversary of the day she had finally allowed the theurgist of Herstal, whom some called witch, to cut open her leg and dig out the splinter of wodeglass. She remembered even now how the bloody sliver had glistened as Ude held it up to the light. Such a small thing, so deadly, a mere fleck of the sleek stone that had exploded in her hand when she picked it up. Wodeglass, it was said, sprang from the otherworld, the tears of the lost and lorn cooled into fist-sized stones dense with bitterness and grief. And beautiful. Irresistible. Even in pieces. That tiny speck of stone had filled her with hot dark dreams of power. If it had not been for Ude, its glamour would have seduced her. It almost did. Even now sometimes she smelled strange scents, or heard sounds, tasted flavours others did not. And so she had left, left Ude and the Empire, left Herstal, and set sail for Dumnet.

The *Mermaid* tacked north, past the hook of rock that was the tip of the island, then swung south and west past the slap and hiss of spray and into the natural harbour carved into the side of the cliffs by wave and wind and smoothed by the river Guer. Evening sun poured past the old fort solitary on its hill and over the roofs of Guerent, tipping them with brass.

The ship nosed alongside an uneven stone quay. Anya picked up the case containing her lute and drum, hung it crosswise over her shoulder and swung herself over the side. The ship bobbed a little as she went down the ladder. Sand scrunched and gritted under her sandals and she staggered a little, surprised by the solidity of the quay.

Guerent looked to be a solid, bustling settlement, extending beyond the houses set into the cliffside. She started to walk.

Her shadow was noticeably longer by the time she found a place to spend the night. The Gate Tavern lay in the northeast quarter of the town, not far from the wall but not near any gate that she could see. The owner, a thin, harassed-looking man who introduced himself as Annic, listened, looked her up and down, and nodded. But he shook his head at her Empire coin. "That's not much use to me." He looked meaningfully at her case.

Anya was tired. "Perhaps you'll take my coin for tonight, and I'll sing for your guests tomorrow."

"I need someone tonight."

"I'm bone weary."

"Then you'll be glad of a good bed. Look lass, you'll not need to do too much, and I'll give you your bed for free tonight, with my Bess's best supper thrown in."

He was the first Dumnetian she had met and she did not know what kind of people they were, but this one, at least, was stubborn. She sighed. "Feed me then, and I'll take my drum and lute to the common room."

"Drum? You don't have a harp?"

"No. No harp."

Annic scowled. "What kind of bard doesn't have a harp?"

"I'm not a bard. I'm a player."

He raised both eyebrows and folded his arms. "If you say so." She did not comment. "Well, follow me then." He led her upstairs and along a narrow passageway. "Best room in the house. Player."

It was small, with one tiny window letting in the last of the sunset through its thick, flawed glass. A fire had been laid on the hearth. The stone floor was recently swept, the straw on the pallet looked fresh, and the coarse blankets were neatly folded. There was even a wooden drop latch on the door. The muscles around Anya's eyes and mouth relaxed.

"I'll have Bess make you up something to eat. And I'll send Jenfer with some hot water."

She latched the door after him and sat down slowly on the pallet. Her leg was aching. She rolled up her trews. The scar just below the knee was tight and red. She took a pot of salve from her case and began to rub it gently into the muscle. The scar reminded her of battles fought and those still waiting, of dreams she had on lonely nights. She rubbed some more. The tension under her fingers began to ease and she let out a long sigh. All she wanted to do tonight was eat a large supper and sleep without dreams.

Her spare clothes were packed tightly around the drum and lute. The black tunic and breeches would show the fewest travel creases. She shook them out carefully and laid them on the pallet. The matching scarf would be at the bottom; she began to unpack, methodically folding clothes, setting aside the scarf, laying packets of herbs and pots of salve on the sill by the pallet. The lute came out last. She ran her fingers over the strings, listening, then began to tune it.

The door latch rattled. "Your water's hot and ready, miss." The voice, muffled by the thick planking, sounded young and impatient. Anya went to the door and lifted the latch. The girl, Jenfer, pushed past with a bowl and pitcher of steaming water. Several clean cloths hung over her arm. "Where do you want it?" Then she stopped, staring at the lute dangling from Anya's left hand.

"On the floor by the pallet will be fine." Jenfer did not move. "The water, on the floor by the pallet, please."

Jenfer, flustered, hurried to do as she was told. She spilled some of the water as she bent down. It splashed warmly on Anya's leg.

The girl's eyes widened and she looked very young and scared. "Sorry! I'm sorry!"

"It's just water." But Jenfer was trembling. Anya sighed. "Put the bowl down, then give me one of those cloths." The girl did, and Anya bent to wipe up the spill. "The number of times I've had to do this when I knocked over the pail I was catching milk in." She gave the floor one last wipe. "There, that should do it." She stood up and gave the cloth back to Jenfer, who just stood there. "Thank you for bringing the water," Anya said patiently. The girl eventually got the message and scuttled out.

Anya closed the door behind her. She took up her lute, plucked a string, listened, tightened it. Jenfer and Annic both thought she was something she was not, and their reactions puzzled her.

#

The common room of the tavern was only half full when Anya checked the top of a table for wine spills and sat down with her lute. She plucked a minor chord. One or two people looked up, then went back to their cups. Annic had not lit a fire: the whitewashed room was as cool as her audience. She shrugged.

She started off with a wordless melody, one she had learned as a child in the village not far from Herstal. It was a simple thing, but she played it with grace and clarity, leaving perfect silences between phrases. From there, she moved straight into a complicated dance melody, elegant and precise. One or two conversations stopped now and again. She took up her drum, tapped it experimentally. She closed her eyes, picking a rhythm from the taut skin as precisely as a cat licks fleas from its kittens. Soft at first, the rhythm penetrated through the low cloud of conversation, like rain. A finger or two released leather cups to tap on tables. She breathed through her nose, feeling blood rush through her arms and fingers, back to her heart, out again. She opened her mouth slightly and began to hum, ruffling the rhythm, blowing it like a wind running over hills and pushing aside tall grass, pulling tatters from the clouds overhead, filling the lungs of people with fresh air, making their eyes sparkle. Her hum climbed up from its bass, wound lazily in between the beats now, teasing. The tempo sharpened and her hands moved like snakes, feinting from the wrists, then striking. Gradually her arms stiffened, driving the rhythm out, beating it from the drum until it swelled and clung to the walls, pulsing like candle shadow. The beat snatched at feet under their tables, lifting sandals, boots, bare heels, dropping them again, lifting. Her hum became more explosive, punching in and out between beats. By the door, Jenfer had her eyes closed and her fingers tapped a pitcher of ale. Anya raised the beat. Louder. Fiercer. Then she stopped.

She surveyed her audience. They were silent. Jenfer blinked and hurried to fill cups; her movement broke the quiet. Several palms beat on the table in appreciation. Anya picked up her lute again. Now that she had them, she would sing.

Afterwards, Anya lifted the hem of her tunic and wiped her forehead. She watched while Annic, Bess, and Jenfer mopped up wine dregs and pushed benches back against the wall. She was too tired to move.

Annic brought her a cup of ale. She sipped at it slowly; what she really wanted was water, cold water.

The tavern keeper smiled. It creased his forehead into thin worms of flesh. "This place will be full tomorrow." He nodded briskly to himself. "Full. And I need the business, I don't mind telling you. So how long will you be willing to stay and play?"

"We'll talk tomorrow."

"You'll at least do one more night? Of course, I'll expect to pay you. As well as give you your room and board." He bent down a little until his face was level with hers. "At least one more night?"

A town this size would be more than enough to keep her busy for one day. She nodded. "But we'll talk more tomorrow."

#

The courtyard was sunny, the air sharp with bruised herbs and the faint sour smell of chickens. Anya sat half in the shade and ate the last of her breakfast apple. Guerent waited.

She headed upland, moving along cobbled streets, then hard packed dirt with a few stones set in it for foot travellers, then a grassy track, until she was standing before the fort overlooking the town. From up here it was plain that long ago Guerent had been two separate settlements, one on the right bank of the Guer, one on the cliffs to the left of the natural harbour. Where the two merged, a wide thoroughfare had grown; that thoroughfare was now the town, lined with the stalls of artisans measuring the feet of rich merchants and displaying supple leathers and bolts of closely woven cloth.

She breathed deep. On the high breeze she could smell the sea and sun-dusted grass. A curlew flicked its wing as it swooped behind a gorse bush. Its cry and the wind hissing through the grass were the only sounds. She stood there, alone on the hill, and let the peace and the sunshine warm her bones.

The fort was abandoned, but not old—built two or three generations ago, at most. Weeds grew bright and undisturbed at the base of its thick walls. The side gate was open. She laid her hand on the wood; it was oak, strong and well-seasoned, and warm to her touch. The iron bands were only just beginning to rust. The fort had been well kept; except for the overgrown courtyard everything was still tidy. She wondered why the grass was not cropped by sheep.

She sat down by a patch of cowslips and closed her eyes, just listening and feeling the sun on her face. After a while she opened her eyes and blinked. There was something. Not wode taint, but . . . something. It lay bedrock deep, clean and strong. That strength could be dangerous if played with, but it did not have the same lorn and terrible power of wodebreath.

A cloud moved across the sun, and she shivered.

#

Annic's brow creased as if he had not heard right. "A whole seven nights?" Anya nodded. He smiled, then caught himself. "Now, your room's satisfactory?"

"It is."

"And the service?"

"Excellent."

"Good. Good. That just leaves the question of the fee." Emotions chased themselves across his face. Proprietor's shrewdness won over any awe he might feel for bards. "Of course, you might not be able to pack them in for seven nights in a row. You'll be old news after a while."

"If I wasn't playing for you, how much would you charge for my room and two good meals a day?"

Annic rubbed at his ear. "Well, it's the best room in the house, and you've been getting good meals." She watched him calculate, then up the cost in the hope that she might ask less as additional fee. "I'd say four shillings a day."

"Then the fee I shall ask will be the same. An additional four shillings for each of the seven nights."

Annic counted surreptitiously on his fingers, judging twenty-eight shillings against the extra custom. The answer was close enough to make him hesitate, but not for too long.

#

On the sixth night a man with one eyebrow and a burn scar for the other stepped over to her table in between songs. He was a head taller than her.

"You're not from here." His voice was hoarse. Perhaps he had breathed the fire that took his eyebrow. "Who taught you?" More demand than question.

She put down her cup. "I've had many teachers, who taught me many things. My mother taught me to milk a cow, my sister to darn hose, my father to build a good fire, even with damp wood. My mother's mother showed me the healing herbs and how to splint a broken bone." The man stirred impatiently. She shrugged. "Clearer questions get you better answers."

"Who taught you to play, and where?" He coughed carefully, into his hand.

"I don't know who you are, or even what you call yourself."

"You may call me Dev."

"Well, Dev, I learned pipe, drum, voice, lute, and harp from my family and the village players as I grew up. Since I left home, I have not been too proud to learn where I could."

He folded his arms; his jerkin parted just enough to show the hilt of a well-used knife at his belt.

"Those who play without the approval of Macalla are ill-advised to practice their craft in Dumnet." He smiled. The scar brow rucked into lumps. No doubt he thought it frightening. "But you're a foreigner. There'll be no penalty if you leave first thing."

"And who is Macalla?"

He coughed again. "Leave first thing. Do you understand?"

She regarded him steadily. "I understand."

He nodded and made his way between the crowded tables and out the door.

Later, when Annic was clearing away, she asked him to send Jenfer to her room with some hot water and warm milk. She was on the pallet, combing her hair, when Jenfer tapped at the door. This time, the girl waited.

"Come in," Anya called. "Put that on the floor, please." At least she no longer looked scared out of her wits. "When you've done that, come and sit. I want to ask you some questions." The comb caught in her hair. A knot. She tugged harder and hissed.

"You're just making it worse," Jenfer said. "Do you want me to do it?"

Anya put down the comb gratefully. Jenfer sat next to her on the pallet.

"Turn this way, so I can have a look." She teased at the knot with gentle fingers. "It's quite tight. Looks like . . . yes. Here." She held out her palm. "See? You had a burr stuck in it. How'd you manage that? Pass me the comb." Anya was amused at the speed with which this girl went from timid servant to bossy older sister. "I used to comb my sister's hair. It was longer than yours, though not so thick. Or so dry. But I expect that's the sea air. I've never been to sea." She transferred the comb to her other hand and started combing with long, strong strokes. "Where are you from?"

"Near Herstal." Jenfer would not have heard of the tiny village of Drenich. "The Empire." She felt Jenfer nod.

"Tell me what it's like. I mean, if you please."

"I'll tell you some stories of Herstal, of Altberg and the Emperor, if you tell me about Dumnet."

"But I don't know anything interesting! I've never lived anywhere but this place," she waved the comb.

"It would be interesting to me. Tell me about the fort, and about bards."

#

The moon was thin and appeared only now and again from behind thick cloud. Anya watched for it through the small panes. Somewhere a dog barked.

According to Jenfer, the man who called himself Dev was not a bard, not a proper one, anyhow. Real bards, as Jenfer was sure Anya knew, were subtle and sorcerous, and advisors to kings. There were precious few in Dumnet until Airget of the Tuatha had crossed the sea with her former betrothed, Macalla, to marry Rufus and become queen. The queen kept Macalla close by her, as advisor. Out of guilt, probably. Now, of course, there were plenty who called themselves bards—who played a bit of music and talked loud about how Dana-the-mother was the only god . . . But they weren't like they were supposed to be in the songs—powerful people, otherworldly—or so she'd heard. She'd never seen one herself. She'd thought Anya was one—she had that look the songs told of: strange and terrible around the eyes, but kind. And she played music like a sorcerer. Dangerous? Well, she wouldn't like to cross one: they owed allegiance to Macalla and he was a very powerful man. The fort? Well now, that was a tale. It had been the old king's grandfather, Leonides, who had moved the court from the ancient capital, Buiscolloc, to the country's centre of trade with the Empire, Guerent. Her grandmother said it had been fine times here then. But then ten years ago, not long after Rufus married Airget and the old king died, they moved everything back to Buiscolloc. Prince Edric was born there. Jenfer's gran said that the Tuatha princess—the queen she supposed she was, really—had refused to spend even a single night in the royal fort here in Guerent. Called it an abomination, she had; said that a sacred grove had been cut down to build the fort. She actually wept. Imagine that, a grown woman weeping over a few trees that had been cut down before her own mother was born! And then when they'd moved the court, Macalla had forbidden anyone from setting foot inside the fort on pain of death. The winter court? In Buiscolloc of course. They'd all be in Buiscolloc: Macalla, Rufus, Airget.

A cloud scudded across the moon. Anya lay back and looked at the ceiling. Rufus and Airget. Airget and Macalla. Macalla and his hireling, Dev.

She fell asleep and dreamed of sitting in the moonlight on the grass of the fort, with Ude behind her, combing her hair.

That dream drew her back to the fort the next day. The main gate creaked in the breeze that drove heavy cloud across the afternoon sky. The cowslips, so bright on previous visits, were muted under the overcast. The grass smelled dank and cold. Anya stood, feet wide apart and eyes closed, oblivious.

Through the earth, something called to her, sang through her blood, whispered under her skin. It sang a song of lament; under the melody lay a deep harmony, an ancient resonance that had sounded through ages. It was the breath of the earth. She listened a long time.

#

On her last night at the Gate Tavern, Anya shared the song of the earth with her audience, breathing it into every drum beat, every touch of lute string; she brought it into every turn of her head and every pause between notes. Through her, the earth sang, and the common room was silent except for her music and the slow breath of five dozen people.

When she finished, there was no applause. Several people blinked and many made the palm-to-heart gesture of respect before draining their cups and leaving.

Anya watched. She felt very calm, very peaceful, even though she knew one of those moving through the door would report to Dev.

Annic came to her table and put a plump coin pouch next to her case. “They didn’t spend much tonight, but I count myself honoured.” He looked at her thoughtfully. “If you don’t want folk to name you bard, then you’d best not play like one.” He turned to leave.

“Annic.” He stopped. “Annic, I’ll be leaving just after the moon sets tonight. It might be safer if you barred your doors after me and slept lightly.”

She watched him decide not to ask questions. “You’ll need something to eat before you go.” He looked at her a long moment. “I’ll see to it myself.”

She was still in the common room, deserted now, when he

brought her bread and fruit and cheese on an old wooden tray. He sat down and lifted a small canvas sack onto the table. "There's more in here." Inside was a hard cheese, two loaves, several apples and a leather bottle. "No doubt you'll be wanting to avoid the well-travelled roads for a while."

She pulled out some coins but he waved them away. "Not this time. I've not heard music like yours since I was too young for a beard, and that from a man so old even his sons will be dead by now. I was beginning to wonder if there were any of you left." He held up his hand. "Oh, I know, you say you're not a bard, and I won't go telling folk otherwise, if that's your wish. But there are those who were here tonight that might."

Anya picked up an apple. It was small and russet-coloured, and cool in her hand. "Thank you."

He nodded and pushed himself away from the table. At the door he paused, one hand on the latch. "Do you have any roads in mind?"

"No. But I'll be heading for Buiscolloc."

"If you want to travel quietly, take the west gate, then follow the track back around the city wall eastward into the forest. Travel that for ten or fifteen leagues before turning south for the capital. Most folk would take the south gate, then the southeast road over the downs."

#

She walked through the night and half the morning. Sweat lay in a fine sheen across her forehead by the time she heard water bubbling over rock and followed the sound to a stream. It moved fast enough, and there were beetles skating across the surface where the beginnings of a pond rippled behind a tumble of boulders. She drank.

The air was still and warm; a butterfly lifted and fluttered past, a handspan from her face. The grass was dry. She curled up in the sunshine and slept.

The stream sang through a dream where she was naked, lying in hot sun, a sun far hotter than this day's, a sun of other days. The world was newer, fresher, and life was lived closer to the ground, nearer to the earth. She had long hair, tangled, and her limbs felt heavy and relaxed, as though she had come from love, or a soak in a hot spring.

She lay face down, fingers digging into the moss, listening to the whisper of the water, the murmur of the wind in the trees, letting the Mother sing to her of the Great Marriage between king and earth in the Long Ago.

She woke on her stomach, her fingers wound in the grass. Every muscle was loose and warm. She lay there a moment, enjoying the sun on her back and the moss under her cheek. She sat up and ran a hand through her hair, remembering the dark, long tangles, and the song of her dream. It was stately, ancient. She wondered what it was called, and who had written it so long ago. Great Marriage. She rolled the phrase around her mouth, tasting it: no wode taint. An old ritual engaged in . . . willingly? Willingly.

First the song of the earth at the fort at Guerent, now a dream of the Great Marriage. Was this why she was here?

It was midafternoon, later than she had intended to sleep. Her neck and leg itched with midge bites. She transferred the knife from her boot to the sheath at her belt. There might be other predators in the wood besides Dev.

The sun was turning from gold to red when she saw the faint track leading left from the main path. She looked this way and that, then followed it.

It ended in a clearing. In the centre stood a house with walls no taller than she; the door, which was closed, came only to her shoulder. She smelled woodsmoke, and a chicken clucked from the undergrowth to the left, but there was no other sound, no birds, no squirrels: someone was hiding inside.

She unslung her case and settled cross-legged in plain sight of anyone who might be peering from the cracks between the wattling. She took out her lute and strummed it gently.

"I mean you no harm," she said, "I'm a singer, travelling here and there. I'd be grateful for a roof over my head tonight and a fire to warm my feet by." Idly, she played the first part of the ancient tune she had learned from her dream. "Of course, I'll be willing to work for your hospitality. I can cut or gather wood, I can cook, or look for the eggs laid by your fowl yonder."

She picked out a melody from the chords she was playing, and began to hum. After a while she forgot to watch the door, and concentrated on the sound she was making, the way it poured rich and strong from her throat and under her fingers.

When she looked up, a child, a girl wearing nothing but torn breeches, stood half in and half out of the door. Anya smiled at her but did not stop playing. The girl edged out from the door and closed it behind her. Anya swung into a different tune, a light, easy-to-learn melody that would appeal to her audience.

The youngster tilted her head. "My da tried to teach me to play, but my hands aren't quick enough anymore."

She held out her hands and Anya stopped playing to look. The girl was eight or nine years old but her hands had seen enough brutal work with axe and hoe to coarsen them to callused and cracked lumps. "I'm Brigid."

"Does your da live with you?" The girl nodded. "Would he like me to come inside and play where he can hear?"

She nodded again, and waited for Anya to stand up.

The inside of the dwelling was dark but slatted with light coming from the chinks in the walls and shutters; it smelled of old sleeping furs, ash, and herbs. A man was sitting on a sleeping shelf by the far right wall. Light sliced a thin line across his face from forehead to chin. His eyebrows were dark.

"Welcome to my home, such as it is." He did not offer his hand to shake. The light across his face broke and reformed. Anya realised he had smiled. "You're not Dumnetian," he said.

"No."

"Play me something."

His voice was deep and brown, like the song of the earth, and full of yearning; he wanted real music.

She played, and into her music she poured all the pain and joy and loneliness, all the fear and determination she had learned the last year. Last of all, she played the song from her dream but this time with concentration, and with power.

"You play that well," he said. "How did you come to it? No, don't answer that yet." He tilted his head in the same gesture Brigid had used. "You don't know what it is you're playing, do you?"

"Will you tell me?"

Light flickered as he shook his head. "Do you play the harp?"

"I have done, a little."

He nodded over at the wooden chest covered with a blanket. "Look in there."

The harp was cased in otter skin. "Get it out and take a look," he said. She unwrapped it. It was twice the height of a footstool, and heavy for a hand harp. The heel was carved from dark bog oak. Inlaid in the wood was a curious spiral of mother-of-pearl. The strings were made of gold.

"It's a harp that needs to be played, and you might be the one. If you play it well enough, it's yours." His voice was hoarse and dark with strength. "Play it."

She leaned the harp back, resting the inlaid spiral against her breastbone. She closed her eyes and lay her palms flat against the slick buttermetal tension of the strings. The dream tune waited in her fingers. The man had heard it already, but it should be played on a harp. Her hands moved, stately and accurate. On the harp, the melody was simple and authoritative. Between the notes she heard another melody; she hummed it, weaving the low tones in and out cleanly, without touching the harp sounds.

The stings hummed to themselves a while before she laid her hand across them. The man said nothing.

"This is a fine harp," she said. "I didn't do it justice." Sunlight slid along the strings as she laid it aside.

"But you hear things, and it helps you sing them." He leaned back until his face was wholly in shadow. "Where did you hear that blood music?"

It was easy to tell him, then, of the fort and its whisperings, of the Great Marriage in the dream. She could not hear or see him nod, but she knew he listened intently.

"The harp is yours," he said abruptly. "You'll make a good bard."

"Being a bard means something more than just playing music, here in Dumnet. I am not one you would call bard."

He laughed softly. "But you are, and more. Have I not just pronounced you so?" The amusement left his voice, leaving his words heavy and cold, like stones. "You are a bard, Anya Reine, as much as I. Though Macalla, by his actions, diminishes me."

She was afraid, but she did not know what she feared. "I don't understand."

He did not reply. She reached out to touch the harp. It would be heavy to carry through the forest but she would leave everything else behind, if necessary.

"No matter, Macalla will fall in the end," he said, and the amusement was back in his voice. "Wrap the harp and leave now."

The harp seemed lighter, or perhaps just easier to handle. When it was wrapped in its sleek skins, she took off her belt and used it to strap her drum case to the harp. Her knife went back in her boot. There would be no refreshment or rest for her here tonight, and she should leave. She wanted to thank him, but did not know how.

He must have understood. "Listen when the earth speaks, and play the harp well. That will be thanks enough." He seemed tired.

Anya put her hand on the door.

"Avoid Macalla until you're ready," he said from the shadow. "You have what he does not, and his jealousy is dangerous." He held out his arms; light caught and broke over what was left of his hands. Worse than Brigid's; much, much worse. "You should know my name. It is Dagda, Ruad Ro-fhessa."

#

When the question struck her, Anya was back on the main path. How had Dagda known her name?

Ahead, a pinpoint of light grew to orange red and lit the underside of the trees. Poachers. Anya watched from the shadows for a while, then stepped into the light, holding up her weaponless hands, making sure her harp was visible.

The younger of the two men at the fire took up his bow, which was still strung. The older stood and motioned her to the fire. "The night will be cold, soon enough. Join us. There's food if you need it."

"I have a little to share," she said, and sat inside the ring of warmth. Outside the circle a twig broke. "Tell your friend to come back to the fire."

"Cait! It's a bard. Come eat your supper." He turned back to Anya. "She broke that twig on purpose. You'd not have heard her if that's how she'd wanted it." He sat down and reached for the hare roasting over the flames. "I'm Owen. This is my sister-son John."

A woman, younger than Owen, though not as young as John, stepped from the trees, sheathing her knife. Owen nodded in her direction. "Cait, my sister."

"But not John's mother," Cait said. "Is that miserable hare cooked yet?"

They ate the hare with some parsnips John pulled from the fire; they were charred outside, raw inside. Anya felt Cait watching her while she ate. Afterwards, they shared Anya's cheese and a bottle of water.

Owen apologized for the size of the hare and the parsnips. "Things haven't been growing right hereabouts for a year or two."

Cait looked at her appraisingly. "You're used to better, I'm sure."

"This is enough, and welcome."

Shadow on Cait's face shifted as she raised her eyebrows. "It'll not be often you drink plain water, or share such a poor meal with the likes of us."

"I've eaten better today than I did yesterday. And there have been days when I would have been grateful for a crust." She wondered why Cait was so prickly.

"Doesn't Macalla feed his bards anymore?"

"I'm no bard of Macalla's."

Owen and John stirred uncomfortably; Cait spat at the fire. The spittle hissed on hot stone. "No one who still has a harp and calls themself bard stays alive, unless they are Macalla's."

"I am no bard of Macalla's," Anya repeated.

Cait reached for the harp case, slowly, and unfastened the ties. Gold gleamed in the firelight. "This says you're Macalla's."

"It was given to me today by a man who lives not far from here."

"No one lives within a day's walk of here," Owen said.

Anya looked at him. "There's a track, no more than two thousand paces from this clearing. And a house. He has a daughter, Brigid."

John frowned at that but said nothing.

"Show us," Cait said.

"I'm not sure I could find it again. It's dark." And she was tired.

"If there's a trail there, I'll find it. Dark or not." She stood up and unsheathed her knife. "Take me there."

Anya doubted they could hurt her before she could escape into the trees, but that would mean leaving the harp, and her drum case. Cait made her walk first, following behind her so quietly that Anya turned more than once to check she was there.

The moonlight hardly penetrated the forest. It was cold. Anya stumbled several times in the dark; she wondered how either of them would manage to spot even a plainly marked trail.

"It's around here, somewhere."

"Keep moving."

She did, as fast as she dared, to stay warm. After a while Cait stopped. "Here," the poacher said softly, "I've found it." She pointed. "It's very faint. Hasn't been used much in a long, long time, though someone's been along it recently. See where the grass is bent?"

"I walked this way."

Cait ignored her. "We'll follow it."

Again, Anya led. The trail was more overgrown than she remembered.

In the clearing, the moonlight was strong. For a moment, neither of them spoke.

The dwelling in the centre of the clearing was a ruin. It had been a ruin for a long time. An oak, old and strong, grew up through the roof. Anya rubbed absently at the scratches on her forearms and wondered if she was dreaming.

Cait prowled the edges of the clearing. "There's nothing here," she said. "There's been nothing here since before the old king's grandfather was a boy. Longer."

"When I was here today, this was whole." Anya did not understand. This was the right clearing. "I sat right here and played my lute. A girl called Brigid came out and told me her father would like me to play for him. I went inside. I played. The man asked me to play his harp, this harp. I did. He gave it to me, told me . . . some things."

"And I suppose his name was Dagda."

Anya looked at her a long time. "How did you know that?"

#

By the fire, Owen stroked his chin thoughtfully. "Dagda, son of Dana, goddess of the People, the Tuatha De Danaan. He is Ruad Ro-fhessa, lord of perfect knowledge. God made flesh, wandering the world to hear the music mortals made."

For the first time, John spoke. "He was here when the very first bards took up their harps. Some say he taught them. I always wanted to be a bard." He looked at Anya, then across at her harp. "He's the father of music and magic in Dumnet. Brigid is his daughter, Dana come again, the goddess with a harp of golden strings which she uses to call down the fires of destruction and purification." He looked at her again. "Yet you say her hands were crippled, and Dagda gave the harp to you."

Anya looked at the case on which her hand rested. "The harp is real." And Dagda? The fire shifted and creaked. John added another branch. Anya watched the flames leap, remembering Dagda naming her Bard; she remembered her own fear of him, momentary though it had been; she remembered his crippled hands, and Brigid's, and that he had asked something of her. Macalla.

"Where's Macalla now?"

"Macalla? In Buiscolloc, where else?" Cait said. "Buzzing round Airget, waiting for Rufus to fall from the tree."

"The king is sick?"

Owen shook his head. "No, but Dumnet is. Rufus, they say, will make the Great Marriage."

The blood music from her dream sang through her head. She frowned. "Great Marriage?"

"When the king offers his blood to the earth," John said. "To Dana-the-mother, who is always thirsty."

#

She left Owen, John, and Cait the next morning. It was not safe to travel with poachers; Macalla guarded the game in this forest jealously.

When it began to rain, she left the path and crouched under a tree. Another five days walk would see her in Buiscolloc. The king and his court were there, and Macalla.

Rain shook and pattered on the leaves over her head. The moss between her feet smelled cold and wet. Avoid Macalla until you're ready: Dagda's warning had been clear. But ready for what? She touched the tip of one finger to a droplet resting on the surface of the moss, enjoyed the way it gave against her skin. Then she flicked it into oblivion. In the winter court of Dumnet, she would have as much resistance to Macalla as a raindrop.

But Buiscolloc was where she had to go. She had come to Dumnet to find something. Peace, she had thought. Instead, she had found the beginnings of who she could be. The fleck of wodeglass embedded in her leg had awakened a part of her that might have slept until the day she died. Though she had rejected the stone, and its warped power, that place inside was forever awake, and hungry for . . . something. She had groped her way to part of the answer, but there was more. And she would have to find it for herself. Ude could have helped her, perhaps. But Ude was an ocean away.

The only way to learn more was to trust her heart. And that meant going to Buiscolloc. Perhaps she would be ready when she got there, perhaps not, but she would go.

When she lifted the harp onto her shoulder, she noticed something nestling in the depression it had made in the grass. She picked it up: a grey flint as long as her middle finger. An arrowhead. She could see the marks where its maker had shaped the stone; there was a spiral notched on one side, like the one inlaid on her harp. It rested comfortably in her palm. She hefted it, then slipped it into her belt pouch.

It looked like the rain was set in for the day. Nothing unusual at this time of year. Autumn was on its way. That thought brought a sense of urgency she did not understand. She set off briskly.

#

Early on the morning of her fourth day since finding the arrowhead, she heard the mewling of an animal. She unsheathed her knife—bandits had used such traps, before now—and stepped under the trees.

A fox was lying on its side at the base of a rowan tree whose leaves were turning the colour of old blood. Next to the fox, half hidden in a drift of leaves, lay the remains of a vole. Anya put her knife away. The fox watched her approach, then laid its head down. It was too near death to be frightened. She knelt next to it. Its left hind foot was swollen and infected; vole bite. Using a stick, she poked the vole free of its leaf barrow. Breath hissed between her teeth.

The vole was grossly misshapen. Physically warped in a way she knew immediately. This was the work of wode.

She sat back on her haunches for a moment and thought. The muzzle of the fox was caked with dried vomit. There was none of this wode-spoiled creature's flesh inside the fox, then. The only source of taint was the bite.

She lifted her finger in front of the fox's snout to let it sniff, then touched the matted pelt of its left leg, high up. The muscle was tight and hot, but that would heal if she could cut away the poison gathering around the bite below its dew claw. It whined as she stood up.

It took her a while to find the white flowers of wild garlic and dig up two bulbs. Then she cut several strips of moss with her knife. She had no means of knowing when the vole had bitten the fox but the influence of wodeglass was fast; she would have to do what she could now, with no time even for fire.

Using two stones, she crushed half the garlic to a paste and rubbed the rest over her knife blade. Then, from her pouch, she withdrew a bundle of yellow silk tied with a blue ribbon. She unwound it. In the centre nestled a tiny stone vial the size of her fingernail. Tincture of alemb. Rare even in Araby where it was prepared from the spines of a desert plant, it had cost her two gold crowns in Altberg. A year ago, Ude had been there to do the cutting, to hold her muscles still and soothe away the pain with theurgy. She herself was no witch, but she was a healer. No Empire physician would do what she was about to, but she had been a healer long before she got the Altberg seal to prove it. What did it matter that the creature suffering before her was only a fox? She remembered her own suffering clearly.

Using her knife, she cut away the lead seal but did not yet unstopper the bottle. She laid her free hand over the muzzle of the fox until it struggled for breath then, careful to turn away her own head, she flicked out the stopper and held the vial under its nose. It sucked in air bitter with alemb and went limp.

Cutting away rotting flesh was not new for her. She ignored the smell as best she could and concentrated on pulling back the skin to expose the flesh beneath. The tendons did not seem to be infected. The poisoned muscle was reddish grey and spongy; it did not bleed under her blade. She cut until she reached healthy tissue.

She smeared the wound with a handful of garlic, packing the paste in as tightly as she could, then wrapped it with the moss. The strip of blue cloth that held her hair back secured the moss to the fox's leg. She checked her handiwork. It would take the fox a day or so to gnaw through the cloth. The wound should stay covered long enough for the garlic to do its work. She listened to its regular breathing. It would stay limp for a while yet.

Even after all the rains of the past weeks, there were brittle twigs and dead fern to be found under the trees. She made a fire, and as the vole and dead flesh burned she tied back her hair with twine from her pack, then held her knife in the flames until the blade turned black. She stabbed it clean in the turf, then heated it again.

When she turned back to check on the fox, it was gone.

#

The vole and the fox were only the first of the plants and animals she found changed by wodebreath. As she drew near Buiscolloc, the taint grew stronger. The trees thinned; when she ate stew in the house of some poor man, she lifted a carrot on her spoon to find it twisted in strange shapes; the children she passed on the path that had widened to a cart track looked sickly, with pale skins and odd eyes; babies did not thrive and cows were slow to give milk.

Buiscolloc stood high on a plain and alongside the slow, wide curve of a river that ran south to the sea, a day's ride away. Somewhere to the west, on the downs road that a more trusting traveller would have taken from Guerent, lay the plain of towers, huge standing stones rumoured to have been laid in a circle by the gods themselves before time began.

The cart track broadened to a road, and the road became paved on either side; the pavements became thronged. A cold wind pushed along the streets close to the ground. On the outskirts, the people Anya passed looked like farmers going about their secondary profession, trade, leading ox wagons, or herding goats, but always in towards the city loaded with produce, and out of the city purses heavy with coin. As she followed the road, it narrowed again; yards to the left and right were full of livestock and farmers bargaining over sacks of grain. Further in, she saw a tavern, The Wyvern, then another and another. And houses. At first these buildings were low, pleasant looking structures, then they grew crowded, and started to shoulder above each other crooking this way and that in an effort to see the light. The result was dark and twisted rows separated by narrow muddy streets reeking of filth. A pig ran from a side alley. She saw a cutpurse slit open the money pouch of a farmer leaning against the lintel of a tavern, and longed for the forest.

The cutpurse slipped the stolen money into his jerkin and glanced around to see if anyone had noticed. Anya made sure she was not looking, but realised he was staring at her nonetheless. Staring at her harp.

She gave no sign that she had noticed his interest but walked quickly. The next tavern was far enough along the road to be out of sight of the cutpurse. She laid the harp against a wall and covered it with her cloak, then waited for someone to come out. It was a man who looked young enough for this to have been his first drink.

He tried to step around her with a mumbled beg-pardon but she laid a hand on his arm, forcing him to look up.

"Is there a temple of Rhea hereabouts?" The Empire goddess of healing had servants everywhere.

He sniffed and wiped at his nose with his sleeve. The sleeve was already wet, either from his nose or from dragging it through ale slops. "East, there's one east of here somewhere." He coughed and shivered.

"Perhaps you would like to show me the way there, and have one of the sisters look to your health."

He laughed. It was a mean, worldly laugh at odds with his face. "They'll be hard pressed to see to their own health when Rufus is dead and gone."

He would have pushed past her but she moved out of his way too fast.

The temple of Rhea was smaller than she had expected. Nor did it have the usual walls and front courtyard. It was a building faced with stone and roofed with clay tiles, which made it different from its wood and thatch neighbours, but it was poor-looking when compared to the large and graceful temples of Herstal and Altberg.

The entrance was a low passageway of curving brick. The far end was barred and attended by a young cleric with her hood pulled up against the cold. She would not let Anya in.

"We're in retreat."

"I have to see your Mother."

"She isn't seeing anyone. We're in retreat."

"I must see her."

The cleric was becoming impatient. "I'm sorry your visit to Buiscolloc has started with disappointment but if it's a room you need, then find an inn. We are in retreat."

"I understand that you might have reason to be wary of outsiders, but I'm not Dumnetian." She thought of the paper in her pouch that she had carried for many months. "I'm a physician from Herstal."

The cleric raised her eyebrows politely.

Anya put down her harp and opened her belt pouch. "Do you read?"

"I do," the cleric said stiffly.

"Here." She held out the scroll stamped with the blue seal of the Herstal Guild of Physicians.

The cleric pulled it through the bars and untied the silk cord. She mouthed the words as she read. She looked up at Anya, then back at the scroll.

"I need to see your Mother," Anya said again.

"Wait here." Her feet crunched on the gravel path. A fountain pattered somewhere in the distance.

The cleric came back without the scroll but with a large iron key. She opened the gate. Anya followed her along the paths where a few roses still bloomed and wind blew fountain spray in her face. The shutters on the infirmary windows were open; it looked empty. In all the temples of Rhea she had ever been, the infirmaries had always been overflowing.

Bild, the Mother of Rhea's temple in Buiscolloc, was a big-boned woman with a pox-scarred face and coppery brown hair tucked behind her ears. Her grey robe was belted efficiently around the waist. "I don't have much time for conversation. Say what you have to say."

Anya put her harp down and considered. "I need your help."

"What makes you believe I'll give it?"

"I'm a healer, you're a healer. Unless I miss my guess, you too come from the Empire." Bild nodded. "I have been entrusted with a . . . task, of which I will only say this: the one who entrusted me with this task does not love Macalla, nor does he believe in the necessity of Rufus's death."

"You mean the murder of King Rufus, in what these barbarians call a religious ceremony." Bild glared at Anya's harp.

"When Rufus is dead, Macalla and his thugs, his so-called bards who denounce all gods but Dana-the-mother, will rule in all but name in this place, and then what will happen to the temples of Rhea, and Mereut, and Tyr?"

"Does Rufus understand all this and do it willingly?"

Bild laughed, harsh as a clatter of copper pots. "He does what he believes is his duty. Any fool can feel that there's something wrong with the land this last year. Rufus is king. He loves his land, and his queen. She tells him he must make the Great Marriage to appease the land and save the kingdom. She tells him it must be so, because Macalla, the great bard, tells her it is so. They're all fools."

Anya assessed this, went back to something Bild had said earlier. "You say Macalla will run the country when Rufus dies. But what of Edric, and Airget?"

"Edric thinks the sun shines from Macalla's fundament. He's only ten. Airget believes Macalla to be a good and kind man, a bard, endowed with wisdom not granted to ordinary mortals." Bild thrust her hands in her pockets and paced. "Bard, hah. I'm sick of the word. If Macalla is a bard, if any of his thugs are kinder than vipers, then I'm a pimple on a horse's arse." Her face was tight in frustration. "There are people out there, sick people, who need our help, yet they won't come and get it because Macalla the Bard says those who worship other than at the feet of the Mother are evil. We've tried, Rhea knows we've tried, but what superstition won't stifle, Macalla's bully boys will. They're everywhere."

"Do you have no supporters in the court?"

Bild looked surprised. "Of course. Several lords, who remember how things were before Macalla came. And Rufus himself. But how can they fight the evidence of their own senses? It's plain that there is something badly amiss in this land. Macalla has a ready explanation, and thugs to back him up if anyone is foolish enough to doubt his word in public." Bild stopped her pacing and looked at Anya. "So what help is it that you want from me?"

Anya smiled, responding to Bild's directness "I'd like a letter or some other means of introduction from you to one of these lords. I want to go to court."

#

The Earl of Caled had fair hair Anya's length and, like Anya's, tied back from his face. He was clean shaven with eyes the colour of Araby spice. His steward had read the letter furnished by Bild, then taken it up to the Earl who had asked for Anya to be shown into his solar. When she had entered he had given her a long look, then bowed and summoned refreshment for both of them.

"Would you like to hear what Bild has to say about you?" Anya gestured for him to read it out. "'Caled, this is to introduce a woman by the name of Anya Reine. She says she's a healer, and has the Empire seal to prove it. But there's a lot she's not telling. She's dangerous, but I'm not sure to whom. Watch her. And look to your health.'"

A servingman entered with a tray of wine and honey cakes. Caled poured for them both. "Bild, in her blunt way, was right. You are dangerous." He handed her a cup. "A true bard is always . . . unpredictable."

Anya rolled the carefully worked pewter stem between her thumb and forefinger. Sunlight burnished the metal and picked out the tiny pieces of glass set in a pattern around the rim. "And will you have me watched?"

He nodded. "For your own safety. There are others beside me with eyes. Within a day or two, Macalla's people will have heard a whisper of you. I'll watch and see that those whispers are delayed on their journey to his ears." He put down his wine, handed her the plate of cakes. She accepted one. "Can you tell me what you plan to do?"

"For now, I need to see Macalla, and Airget, and Rufus. I need to see how they are. What they're like." She tried to explain. "I have to prepare for something. Though I'm not sure what."

His eyes were wide and gentle with compassion. "I'll do what I can. For now, though, when you're rested, would you do me the honour of playing?"

#

Caled held a feast for the royal couple. Anya dressed herself in servants' clothes and carried heavy trays of game meats and platters of bread from table to table. She was careful to avoid the high table where Rufus and Airget sat with Caled and the other noble guests until she was used to the rhythm of serving. Then she took a jug of the best wine from the kitchens and walked through the hall, up the steps of the dais.

The high table was curved in a crescent so those at either end could, by dint of shouting, converse with each other. Caled sat in the centre, Rufus on his right, Airget on his left. Anya walked to the centre and filled Caled's cup. Rufus was talking to the woman on his right. He was tall, with a large head and hair the colour of a peat bog. He wore an earring of thick and cunningly patterned gold in his left ear but no jewellery on his hands or arms. His eyes were soft blue, like sky washed clear after rain, and matched his clothes. There were lines at the corners of his mouth and eyes. He was not a happy man, though Anya guessed he had been, once.

His cup was huge, of gilded silver, decorated with chips of amethyst and topaz. She poured carefully. He turned to take it from her. In the smoke-heavy light, the rich red wine looked like blood. He looked at it, then at her. She kept her face blank, then allowed confusion to crease her forehead. He sighed and drank, turned back to his companion. Anya edged away from his pain.

Airget wore green, and sat very straight in her high-backed chair. She looked to be of medium height. Her hair, braided and coiled on top of her head, gleamed like polished oak. Her forehead was smooth and relaxed but her eyes were distant. She was not listening to the man seated next to her, though Anya doubted that he knew that. She nodded her thanks to Anya as she filled her cup. She wore a single ring of plain silver on her right hand. She was with child, in the early stages.

Anya stayed at the high table with the wine. Rufus drank lightly; Airget emptied her cup several times but did not seem to be much affected. Players began to tune up in the gallery. Airget lifted her head, waiting, but Rufus did not stop talking until the players began. They were lively, nimble-fingered on lute and pipe and with pleasant enough voices but Airget seemed to lose interest after a few verses. It was a subtle thing; she lowered her lids slightly, touched her cup with a fingernail. The lowered lids made her face long and sad. Anya wondered if she missed the music of the Tuatha, or of the bards. Part of Airget's sadness might be the necessity of the king's death, but it was a gentle sadness, the sadness of a friendship to be lost, not a love to be fiercely protected. Anya wondered if she had ever loved—if she had loved her former betrothed, Macalla.

The wine jug was empty. She took it back to the kitchens but did not pick up another. She had learned all she could for now.

#

The sky was overcast and the solar cold when Anya spoke to Caled the next morning. The same servingman who had brought the wine and cakes that first day was building a fire in the grate in the north wall. Caled's cheeks were bright and his hair windblown. He smelled of leaves.

"Autumn's almost here," she said absently, then closed her eyes against sharp realization. Of course: this autumn, when the fields were ploughed. Behind her closed eyes she saw how it would be, heard the song she had listened to in her dream, the blood music.

She opened her eyes, looked directly at Caled.

"After the harvest they will plough the king's blood into the fields," she said, knowing it to be true. "Macalla will lay him down over a furrow and open his veins until the king's blood runs like a river over the earth and the Mother drinks." She frowned. "But that's not what the Mother wants." She leaned forwards and grasped the earl's wrist. "Caled, that's not the way it should be. Macalla has it wrong. There's something, something else at work here. I don't understand."

Caled tried to shrug. Anya realized she was still gripping his wrist and let go. He rubbed his hand casually enough but she saw the lift in his shoulders and the tight skin around his eyes: she had scared him. Caled was another who could never relax with her enough to become a friend.

The fire in the north grate was smoking; a memory of Ude's room, Ude's bed in the morning when the fire was still only half alight made her grit her teeth against tears. Her next words came out harsh and tight.

"Tell me everything you know about Macalla."

#

She left her harp in the guest room at Caled's, then stepped out into the night. The air was cool and still; her mouth was dry. Just four days to the full moon. Tonight Macalla would be at The Wyvern tavern, as he was at this time every month. For convention's sake, he never announced who he was, though regulars knew. Those players new to Buiscolloc who went there to play did not. The Wyvern was his recruiting ground, Caled said, where any player of any talent would be invited to study with Macalla. Some became the ones who called themselves bards and did Macalla's work, others were never heard of again.

Though Dagda had given her the harp less than a fortnight ago, it felt strange to walk through the streets with only her drum and lute. She found herself wanting to lean slightly to balance a weight that was not there.

The Wyvern was bigger inside than it looked, and crowded. She moved quietly past the people standing at the back and made her way to the left hand wall where she could stand in the shadow cast by a badly smoking torch. It was hot. She unslung her case, put it by her feet, and folded her cloak on top of it. A harried looking man pushed to her side, a jug in each hand.

"Wine or ale?"

"Ale."

He held out a jug. Anya held out her empty hands. The man sighed, pushed his way to a table and reappeared with a cup which he shoved into her hand.

"If you want more, keep hold of the cup." He poured a thin, expert stream of ale. "A penny. Or free if you're going to play." He nodded at the shape under her cloak.

She took a penny from her pouch. "Assume I'll just be listening."

On a raised platform too low to be called a stage, a man was playing the lute. Anya listened. It was all surface melody, and his rhythm was ragged. She searched the crowd for Macalla. She knew him at once by his stillness.

He was at a table at the front of the room, sitting with just five others. They had the whole table for themselves when others were standing or sitting on the floor. There were two harps, uncased, on the floor by their feet. His hair was almost the same brown as her own, light for a Tuatha, twisted into a single braid down his back. He was of medium height, and medium build. He was leaning his chin on his hands and listening to the lute player. From where she stood, Anya could only see him in quarter profile; his cheek rose and his mouth lifted slightly. The lute player looked down and faltered. Anya wondered what Macalla looked like when he smiled.

The lute player finished and climbed down to desultory clapping. A woman holding a set of double pipes took the stage and cleared her throat. Anya watched Macalla watch her. The piper was worse than the lute player. Macalla turned to one of his companions whose face was hidden and whispered something. The pipe player blew on. Macalla's companion nodded and leaned down for his harp. He began to tune it; the clear notes cut across the reedy efforts of the woman on stage, but she continued determinedly. The crowd stirred at the sound of the harp and the man tuning it lifted his head and smiled. One eyebrow shone in the light: the man who had threatened her in Guerent, Dev.

Anya went still. Had he seen her? She breathed deep, filling her lungs and her mouth, then let the breath out slowly. She was in shadow; he would not see her. And she still needed a good look at Macalla.

The woman on stage finished and bowed but no one noticed.

"Ready for more?" It was the man with the ale jugs.

"No. Thank you."

He blocked her view of Macalla. "What do you play?"

"Drum. Lute."

"Are you good? You look like you'd be good. Why not give it a go? And you'd get a free drink." He waved the jug.

"No. Thank you."

"Nervous, eh? That Macalla'd be enough to scare me rigid, too. Here." He plucked the cup from her hand and filled it with the same, expert stream. "My son played here once. He told me what it felt like, waiting. Go on, drink it down." He waited expectantly. Anya drank it. He filled it again. "There now, you drink that one, too, and maybe things won't look so bad." He winked and squeezed his way past her into the crowd.

The sound of the harp had pulled at the audience, rearranging it into new patterns. She had to step a little way out of the shadow to see past them to Macalla's table. The room smelled of sweat and smoke and was hot with noise. It would be hard to fight her way to the door through the crowd.

Macalla stood. Dev handed him the harp. He did not bother to take the stage. Instead, he hitched his hip onto the wine-stained table and rested the harp on his thigh. He bent his head to listen to the ripple he stroked from the strings and his braid fell forwards. He tossed it back and the ruby in his ear glowed hot and red in the torchlight. The crowd pulled taut around him, like a bowstring.

Anya held herself tight, locked the muscles in her legs and arms so that she could not move. Here was the source of the taint that drained the life from Dumnet. The blood in her veins felt thick and sluggish. It was something she recognised. A year ago, before the stone had been cut from her leg, she had struggled sometimes in the night with this soft and dangerous languor. Now something in Macalla called to a part of herself she had thought healed. Perhaps she would never heal, never be free of it.

Macalla began to play, and for Anya the music took dark and dangerous shape. It called to her, promising her a way to use the power she knew she had, a power that no amount of cutting could take from her. All she had to do was embrace it, acknowledge it. Come to him, learn how to use it without losing control to it.

She licked her lips. Somehow, Macalla was using the power of wode, and its presence called to her. But it was a battle she had fought and won before. It was a false promise that Macalla's music made. She tried to sip from her cup. It was slippery with her sweat. She had to hold it with both hands. Remember Dagda's hands, she told herself. Macalla did that. But Dagda wasn't real. Was he? His harp was real. Yes, his harp was real. And he had given it to her; asked her to face Macalla, when she was ready.

Macalla's music filled the room and she could taste his power. She was not ready. What Dagda wanted from her was impossible. She could not face this.

Sweat prickled in the small of her back. Macalla's hands moved easily over his harp. They were strong hands, well cared for; light slid over the glossy fingernails. His eyes were closed. She stared at his lids, wondering how he'd come to this. He could have been a bard.

He opened his eyes and looked straight at her through the crowd.

She only just held herself from bolting.

His gaze passed on. She picked up her case and cloak, slung them over her arm and pushed her way towards the door. In the dark a man blocked her way. He moved clumsily, bumping her shoulder. Anya felt a swift tug at her pouch. She brought one hand down hard on his wrist, made a knuckle with the other and laid it against his throat apple.

"The door," she said quietly, pushing him, moving him quickly. Macalla's song ended. She removed her hand, reached for the latch.

"Where's your harp?"

She turned. In the light by the door she saw it was the same cutpurse who had seen her on the road into Buiscolloc. He was rubbing his throat. She hit him twice; in the stomach just below the ribs and where his neck joined his shoulder. He folded onto the floor with a retch that became a sigh.

She ran through the streets. Macalla had recognised something in her, understood the danger she might represent. He would give chase. At least the cutpurse would be unconscious for a few minutes, long enough for him to be ignored and his knowledge of her harp to be overlooked. It would take Macalla several minutes to organise pursuit. Long enough for her to lose herself.

The sweat on her forehead cooled and the ale lay heavy in her stomach. The splash of her footsteps echoed through the streets. After a few minutes she ducked into an alley where she fastened her cloak around her shoulders and settled her drum case more comfortably on her hip. She ran again.

In the distance a dog barked, then another. She made straight for the nearest light. It was another tavern. She steadied her breathing and walked in, through the drinkers, into the kitchen. It was empty; everyone was busy serving in the common room. She strolled out the back, pulled herself up onto the roof of a low outbuilding and ran, bent low against the moonlight, to where it shouldered onto the main roof. She threw her case up first, then hauled herself onto the thatching. It was slippery with recent rain. The building opposite was close. She jumped, dug her fingers into the thatch to stop herself sliding. Then she ran on, from rooftop to rooftop, not thinking, just moving, leaping, rolling. Running again. When she almost missed a leap, she hunted for another outbuilding, dropped down, rolled, dropped again and staggered as she hit the alley on her feet. She ran on. She kept an easy pace, but fear made her breath ragged.

She slowed to listen and could not hear the dogs. She was safe.

Just to be sure, she took a roundabout route on her way back to Caled's, and trod through rivulets of human filth more than once.

The servingman unbolted the door for her and must immediately have gone for Caled. He strode into the guest apartments, still fastening his robe, as Anya was scooping her clothes into her case.

"Three of them know my face." Her words were swift, deft, like her packing. "I have to go. It's not safe." She tied the smaller case to the larger, and swung them onto her shoulder.

"Wait, I'll have some food brought for you."

"I haven't time." She just wanted to get out, get away from Macalla now, while she still could. The cutpurse might be talking; the dogs may have followed her scent onto the roof, or picked it up in some alley. It was only a matter of time before Macalla put guards on all the roads leading out. If he had not already done so. She gestured at the door Caled was blocking. "I have to go."

"You'll be back?"

She did not answer.

#

By early morning she was in the forest again. She followed a path alongside the river; the trees were too dense, the undergrowth too tangled to allow anything else. The river made her nervous; its rushing water would hide any sound of pursuit. She was tired, tired enough to keep seeing things out of the corner of her eye, and to hear whispering in the roar of the river. She needed to sleep.

Ahead and to the left of the path was a flat piece of land thinly seeded with trees, with a bow of water at its back. Many years ago that bow of water had been a huge lazy curve of river, then one year the water had cut its way through the short neck of the bend and silt had sealed up the slower moving curve until it was a small lake. She would be safe there where the water was quiet enough to let her hear someone before they saw her. The trees, while thin enough to push through, were too thick to see past, if she lay still.

Morning sunlight seeped through the trees like cold yellow wine and the underside of the leaves shimmered with glassy river light. Anya lay on her back and wondered if she was breathing or drowning. Blue and gold streaked past her and splashed, flashed up again with silver in its mouth. Kingfisher. Fisher of kings. Like Macalla, the bird had bright eyes that reflected unrecognisable things and remained unblinking for too long.

Something pawed her arm, breathed on her cheek. She jerked awake. There was nothing there. A dream.

She waited for her heart to slow, then closed her eyes again. Something cold brushed her ear, licked. She leapt to her feet and pulled out her knife. She could see nothing, but whatever it was was still there; she could hear it breathing. It sounded like a small animal. Ahead and to her left, in the direction of the path, a fox yipped. She walked a little way. The yipping came again, close enough for her to be able to see the fox, if it had been there. There was nothing. She sheathed her knife, retraced her steps, picked up her harp.

The yipping moved ahead of her. The path was dark and cold, and she pulled her cloak around her. A dry twig broke under her boot. The sound snapped from tree to tree, making the muscles jump under her skin.

The fox she could not see led her to a straggle-haired woman who stood at a fork in the path, scraping moss into her skirts from the bark of a tree. Although Anya moved quietly, the woman looked up from her work and ran, though not before bundling up her skirts to carry the moss. The fox was silent. Anya followed the woman down the fork.

The dwelling she came to was not easy to distinguish from the one in the clearing where she had spoken to Dagda, not so long ago. It, too, was low with a sagging roof, though this time patched with twigs where the thatch had come loose. No smoke came from the hole in the roof that served as a crude chimney. There were no windows. The single door was shut.

The fox she still could not see scratched at the door and whined.

She walked across the mossy clearing and knocked on the door. Its warped and rotted timbers rattled. In the silence, she imagined she heard laboured breathing. More than one person. She put her palm against the wood and pushed. The door creaked open. She did not step inside.

"I mean no harm." Her only answer was hot and broken breathing from the far wall, and harsh but regular breath from just inside the door, from about shoulder height. The woman. Whoever the other person was, they were too ill to hurt anyone.

Something brushed against her legs as it stepped past her. Claws scraped the floor under the unevenly strewn rushes. She ducked inside. It was close and dim; the only light came from holes in the roof and the open doorway. With the door shut it would be hard to see. Earthy, mossy smells mixed with those of damp, illness, and the body dirt of years.

The sleeping shelf had collapsed a long time ago and the pallet was pushed up against the wall. Its occupant lay under a greasy fur.

"He's dying," the woman said, from the thick brown shadow behind the door. Underneath the dull resentment the voice was younger than Anya had expected.

Still stooped, Anya crossed the floor and knelt on the filthy rushes next to the pallet. It was John. Some of his teeth had been knocked out and one eye was almost closed by a half-healed cut that ran over the eyelid. The other eye stared out bright and hard with fever. His face looked as though some cruel god had taken his hair in one hand and chin in the other and pulled until the flesh stretched too thin. His skin was reddish yellow and hung in loose folds around his neck. He had been fighting the fever for days; it was eating him alive. He would not last much longer.

The woman stepped out into what light there was, held out a handful of moss. "Was going to put this on his leg."

Anya pulled back the fur and looked at the leg. It was tight and swollen above the knee; she closed her nose reflexively against the smell. It could not have happened long after she had left them.

"Where are the others?"

The woman's gaze wandered vaguely around the walls.

"The others," Anya repeated. "What happened to the others?" She changed tactics. "Where did you find him?"

"He's my husband."

The woman was a simpleton. Anya pulled off her cloak and laid it on top of the harp. "I need some light." John's breeches were stretched tight over the swelling. She slid her knife between skin and cloth and slit the material all the way to the thigh. Angry red streaked from the wound and disappeared under his tunic. It was hard to breathe against the loud uncertain rhythm of his breath and the luxuriant rot of his wound.

Shadow flickered on the wall before her: the woman had lit a torch.

"Bring it over here."

She did. "He's dying."

Anya ignored that.

"He's my husband."

"Hold the torch higher please." She cut his breeches all the way to the top and eased them open. His belly was distended. He moaned, then laughed. Moaned again. She laid her fingers against his neck, counted. The pulse was fast and not strong. She leaned over his mouth and sniffed. His breath smelled rotten.

She covered him again and sat back on her heels. She could not cut the rot from his whole body; his pain would get worse, and he would die. Before nightfall; dawn at the latest. John, who had always wanted to be a bard.

"Hold the torch over here." She opened her pouch, looked at the packets tied with silk. All her alemb was gone, used on a fox.

"Fox," John said clearly. His bright eye was focused at the end of the pallet. "White. It's got red ears." He laughed. "Fox."

"Been seeing things for days," the woman said, waving her torch over his feet. Anya thought she saw something, but it could have been the lurching flame shadow.

"Please keep the light still."

John giggled. "He's got a cold nose." He tilted his head a little, stared at nothing, then turned his eye to Anya. "He wants you to sing."

Anya looked down at her packets. The fox wanted her to sing. Was this delirium, or something else? She lifted her head and met his piercing stare. "And you, John," she asked gently, "would you like me to sing?"

He smiled: he did not hear her. She turned to the woman. "I'll sing for him. He seems to wish it. But first I'll do what I can to ease his pain. I'll need fresh water. Cold will do."

The woman pushed the butt of the torch into the dirt near the doorway and left carrying a wooden bowl. The torch flame smoked and swayed this way and that. Anya unwrapped her harp and tuned it, then untied two packets and tipped one into the other. She stirred the mixture, a brittle dark-green herb and a brownish powder, with her finger. It would blunt the edge of his pain, no more. If she could get him to swallow it.

The woman was gone a long time. She carried the bowl in both hands and water dripped from between her fingers.

"Do you have anything that doesn't leak? Something smaller."

"A cup?"

"A cup would be very good."

Anya untied the scarf from her arm and used it to wipe the inside of the cup. She tipped in the contents of her packet, added some water, then stirred it with her finger again.

"We have to get him to sit up and swallow this."

"He can't sit up."

"No, we'll have to help him. Leave the torch where it is and hold his head. Hold him steady."

John thrashed as the woman pulled him to a half-sitting position and locked her arm around his neck. Anya held the cup to his lips. He turned his head away, knocking the cup, almost spilling it.

"John, try to drink it, John." She doubted he heard. She turned to the woman. "Hold him steady."

"No!" John shouted, whipping his head back and forth like a snake. He stopped so abruptly that Anya thought he was having a seizure. "Ow. My ear. Don't bite." He whimpered, but held his head still.

"Now hold him." The woman tightened her grip and Anya held his nose until he opened his mouth. Expertly, she tipped the liquid past his tongue, closed his mouth and stroked his throat until she felt him swallow. "Ease him down onto the bed."

His eye flicked open. "Sing," he said, "the fox is waiting for you."

She stroked his head until his breathing eased; he lay quietly. The torch was guttering; the fingers of shadow had become thick arms gliding sinuous and smooth over the floor, the fur, the harp. Its strings glowed hot and red as she leaned it back against her chest.

The fox is waiting for you.

She laid her hands against the strings and closed her eyes, flicked them open again in surprise. She closed them again, tentatively.

The fox was white, as John had said, with ears that were red on the inside. It was sitting on his chest. Anya wondered how he could breathe. She opened her eyes and stared directly at John. There was nothing on his chest. She closed her eyes again, and there it was. It was waiting for her. She did not understand, but it was waiting for her to play. Was John doing this somehow?

She plucked the strings gently, groping for what she should play. Something to soothe the fever, ease John's pain. She curled her fingers into a wide claw and pulled a dissonant chord from the gold, listening to the way it crept through the thick shadows and seeped through the fur and lay on the hot skin of the dying man. She flicked at the strings again, this time with a twist at the end of the chord, and felt the music gather around the head of the torch. She did not understand what was happening, but the fox looked at her, listening. For John, then. Her hands licked over the strings without rhythm, like tongues of flame. The torch fire stretched then leaned towards her, brightening from dull red to orange to yellow then yellow white, drawing strength from her music. Bright fire, cleansing fire.

As the flame burned brighter and her hands moved faster she moved further away from herself until she was floating in a cool and distant place, watching her kneeling self play for the life of a man she barely knew.

The fox floated next to her. She turned to it. In the cool blue light its fur was silver rather than white. It looked at her with Dagda's eyes.

"Was it you all along, then?" It licked its flank. "What is this place?"

The fox swelled, grew indistinct, shimmered into the form of Dagda. His hands were still crippled, but some of the gashes were healed to pink scars, and two of his fingers were straight now.

"This is the place to which you must come when you call those who will aid you."

"I don't understand." She did not understand any of it.

"You will. For now, listen. The earth is being strangled and starved. It is Macalla's doing. You must stop him, and stop the wodebreath he pulls into this world with his hunger for power. Then the royal family must make reparation, but not in the way Macalla intends. The king must not die, or Macalla and wode will triumph."

"But . . ."

He shimmered. "You must stop Macalla."

The fox was beside her once again. It looked at her with silvery pink eyes.

"Dagda?"

Dagda spoke in her head. "This is Vuhs. Learn to understand him and listen to his warnings. He is yours, though no gift of mine. In a way, he is you, a part of you that can move ahead and see in places you have yet to visit."

And she was back under the broken roof, bowed over her harp, the strings vibrating gently against her fingertips. The air smelled scorched.

Although the torch was out, the hut was lighter than it had been: afternoon sunlight slanted through the door that stood wide on its hinges. There was no sign of the woman.

John was breathing easily. She held onto her harp for a moment, listening. He was not asleep. She looked up.

He was looking at her through one wide eye and one drooping eye. She had seen a child look that way after dropping a precious glass bowl that by some miracle did not break.

"When we met you in the forest, I thought that for all your strange story you were just a girl. Are you real?"

In reply, she stretched out her hand so he could reach for it. It was an effort to move. He touched the back of her hand to reassure himself, then withdrew. His fingers were warm but not fevered.

She pulled herself to her feet. "Let me see your leg." He drew back the fur and she looked for a long time at the neatly cauterized wound surrounded by healthy skin.

"Tell me what happened." He stared at her. She took his hand in her own. "Please. Tell me what happened to you, and to Cait and Owen, and then tell me what happened here, just now." Her voice wobbled.

"A trap. Macalla's men broke the leg of a deer, and waited. We followed its spoor into an ambush. They— Cait and Owen are dead. They must have thought I was dead too. When I came to, this mad woman was tugging at me. She got me here, somehow."

Anya looked around. "Where did she go?"

"She ran off when you, when it . . ." He trailed off, his eyes wide.

"I need to know, John. Please."

After a moment he started to speak in a low voice. "I don't know how much was fever dream. There was a fox. Or I thought there was a fox. It bit my ear, made me hold still. Then you were playing and you—" He lifted his hand and hers, let them drop again. "It was like you sucked the fire from the torch and it burned all over you, then another you stepped out. Only you were still playing your harp. There were two of you. The fire-she came over here and, and lay on top of me. You, she, kissed me, burned me some." He pointed. There were blisters around his mouth. His bottom lip was puffy. "Then the fire-she breathed into me. Ah, it burned. It burned like nothing I know of. Burned in my lungs and my bones and my blood. Just burned and burned. Burned the fever right out of me." He nodded to himself. "Surprised the whole place didn't go up." He glanced at the wall. Anya thought she could see scorch marks. "Then the fire-she sucked her breath out of me again, and took away all the pain and the poison. She laid her hand on my leg and I screamed. When I opened my eyes again, there was just you." He looked at her curiously, less afraid now. "This has never happened to you before, has it?"

She shook her head. "Lie back and rest now. I'll bind that leg for you. You'll need to keep it clean."

He lay back obediently, but she just sat for a while, too tired to move. She closed her eyes. Vuhs sat just beyond the door, licking his leg. She opened her eyes again. "The woman seems to be under the illusion that you're her husband."

"I know."

"Will she care for you? There's something I must do."

He nodded, then hesitated. "Cait and Owen need burying. I'm likely to be here some time. They're an hour's walk from here." She said nothing. "They need burying."

She sighed, then nodded and got to her feet to tend to his leg.

She was tying off a rough dressing when the woman came back. Anya straightened. "Keep the wound clean and change the dressing every day," she said, ignoring the woman's terrified stare. "If you have it, feed him broth tonight and something solid tomorrow." She turned back to John. "Rest as long as you can."

She picked up her harp and turned to the door. The woman cowered back against the wall. Anya walked past her, out into the dusk; from the corner of her eye she caught a flash of silver white. It followed her as she walked along beside the river.

The air was cool and fresh, a breeze sighed through the leaves overhead making them rustle and whisper; autumn was drying them to golds and reds.

She had healed a man by calling fire.

She stood still and closed her eyes. She found herself in the cool blue place. From here, she saw things differently, and understood. Vuhs chased a leaf along the path, through air that was playful, alive. Alongside her, the river sang and threw itself over rocks, swirled its skirts and ran on; the water was alive. Beneath her feet she could feel the cold strength of rock and earth, living and breathing. Beyond the thunderclouds gathering above the trees flickered lightning, a fire she could call to her, just as she had called flame from the torch. Air, fire, water, and earth, all alive. Dagda had helped her see: this was who she was, a woman who could call on the power of the living world. The price he asked was that she face Macalla.

But first she had some graves to dig.

#

The night was soft, silent but for the scuff of her boots on the dry grass as Vuhs led her further up the hillside. Below, the rooftops of Buiscolloc lay slippery in a puddle of moonlight; the moon was full. Her breath was warm and ragged, though she carried nothing but her harp, its strings bared to the still air. The arrowhead she had found in the forest lay beneath the scarf wrapped around her left biceps. Every time she moved her arm it pressed into her skin.

Clouds slid between the moon and the hillside. She followed the silver flash of Vuhs as he wound around the rise to approach the hilltop from the side opposite the city. She crept forwards and crouched behind a hummock.

The hilltop was crowned with a circle of stones. Some had fallen and it was apparent from their length that the ones still standing showed only half their height. Granules of mica and quartz glittered in the light of a dozen torches held by some of the people who stood inside the circle. She recognised Caled, and the one who called himself Dev.

Inside these torchbearers and observers stood a group of three: Rufus and Macalla wore white, Airget green.

Ploughed through the centre of the turf, lying between the trio and Anya's hiding place, was a deep furrow: rich dark earth lay turned back against the green, waiting. The air tasted damp and loamy.

Macalla lifted his hand and the crowd, already silent, watched as he extended it to Rufus. Rufus looked briefly at his queen before taking it. They stepped away from Airget, and across the gash, then turned to face away from Anya and back towards the queen. The king was bare of jewellery. Prince Edric, looking cool and distant, stood between two young men. The king's gold gleamed at his ear now.

Macalla released Rufus. This time when he lifted his hand, it held a knife of dark wood and stone. Rufus went down on one knee. He knelt on a clod of earth. An old scar above his elbow reflected pale in the torchlight. His hair gleamed. Macalla, expressionless, looked at him awhile.

He raised the knife again. Movement rippled through the watchers as their eyes fixed upon the blade. Anya studied it. One side glinted wetly, like jet. Wodeglass. But it no longer had the power to call her: she knew who she was. Macalla paused, then stepped to Rufus's side and laid a hand between the king's shoulders. He pushed gently, until the King leaned out over the gaping furrow, throat extended.

Anya stood and stepped into the circle of torchlight.

Macalla met her eyes as he had before, and recognised her.

"You won't be using that knife tonight," she said, not taking her eyes from him. He looked away briefly, at one of the watchers, then turned back. He smiled.

A sword scraped from its scabbard. Dev stepped towards her, blade held low. Anya regarded him steadily. From behind her, another sword rasped free in her defence. Caled.

"There will be no blood shed in this circle," she whispered to the air pooling around the ankles of Caled and Dev. They stumbled on the smooth turf. Then she turned her gaze to Macalla. "Dagda gave me a message from Dana-his-mother. I will sing it for you."

She sat down on the turf, cold and damp through her trousers, and leaned the harp up against her chest.

She looked up at him. "You see, the mother of this world doesn't want what you want to give her. It is another power entirely that wishes for the death of the king and the confusion of the queen. Do you know what that power is, Macalla? Do you even know why the bards of the Tuatha refused to teach you?"

"They did not refuse. I am a bard."

"No. Though you have talent." He glanced over at the queen. Ah . . . All those dreams Dagda had sent, all the things she had learned, from Cait and Owen, from Annic, from Jenfer. She understood now. "You want the queen, but the queen doesn't want you. She wants what you could have been. You lied to her." She spoke softly, so only the two of them would hear.

He said nothing, but now he held the knife in both hands, pointed out, at Anya.

"You could have been a bard, but that would not have been enough for you. It would never have been enough. And now the power that flows through you when you play, when you whisper to the queen of the old ways and speak to the king of his duty to his people, that power does not belong here. It uses you. You serve it. The knife you hold is its knife; the stone set in the blade is its stone, its door in. Macalla, there is still time to refuse it."

The veins in his arms rippled like snakes as he gripped the knife. Without taking his eyes from her, he stepped backwards towards Rufus. "The earth shall drink tonight."

"No." She was implacable.

"Yes." His voice was low and clotted with effort. He lifted the knife and pushed the glistening point into the flesh at the base of his thumb. He breathed heavily, then laughed. Anya heard the power in that laugh. "Yes," he said again, and this time he spoke lightly, easily, "She will drink twice. From the king, and then from you."

The moon slid free of cloud and the hot glow of torchlight cooled to silver. Blood ran freely down Macalla's arm and dripped onto the turf. She watched one drop hit the tip of a blade of grass, then run stickily down to the root. In the quicksilver light it looked black. Macalla laughed and dug the knife deeper into his hand. The air above him deepened and thickened; under its tarnish, the skin of the watchers looked coarse and grainy. Someone gasped, but then Anya had no more time to think: the air was swarming.

It hummed over her, rusting the blade of her knife, shrivelling the leather of her shoes. The stitching of her clothes rotted, and she understood why the strings of her harp were of gold, the imperishable metal. Wode could speed time, age materials to rubbish between heartbeats. But gold was imperishable, and the bog oak already thousands of years old.

She ran her fingers over the strings, lovingly, easily as dust settling. Cold gathered under her where she sat. It collected around the point where the spiral carving on the harp lay against her breastbone, and beneath the scarf wrapped around her left biceps.

Macalla looked up at the sky and opened his mouth. "Come!" And he drew in great tearing chunks of air, air full of the hot dark breath of wode that flocked to the glass buried in his blade. It filled him and made him strong. He bent his gaze upon Anya.

Her fingers hissed against the strings now, harsh as a sandstorm. Cold seeped up from the bedrock and bit deep into her breast and arm. Not fire to answer Macalla, but the sleeping strength of the earth. She sang it out, driving a cold wedge through the heat surrounding him, in until it touched the wound in his hand and sealed it. He faltered.

Her music rained upon Macalla, bruising him like pebbles. She hummed and it became a deep subterranean vibration. One of the fallen stones broke with a sharp crack. The ground trembled.

Clouds moved across the sky and cupped the hill in darkness. Macalla's teeth gleamed red in the torchlight as he spat skin ripped from his wrist. Through the music, Anya heard blood spatter on the grass. She breathed deep and rolled her music across the turf, grinding, inexorable. It sealed the furrow, like a hand smoothing sand.

Her music surrounded Macalla now, trapping him, but his blood was still hot with wode. She played slowly, strongly, calling the earth. Deep beneath her, rock groaned. The cold at her breast and biceps burned and tendons tightened in her neck and shoulders as she tore magic from the body of the earth. Between her and Macalla, the ground rumbled and shook. The turf split, pushing forth a mound the colour and texture of wormcast. Behind Macalla, another mound of earth rose and next to him another, and another, until earth pressed at him from all sides. The cold at Anya's breast and arm was agony. Macalla beat at the earth with his fist but the mounds grew and pushed inwards until only his head and chest showed.

He stabbed at the rampart of earth. The knife exploded. Earth crept up his arm to his collarbone.

Anya breathed steadily, in and out, keeping a rhythm with the music she stroked lightly now from the golden strings. The moon came out.

Airget took one step forwards. "Stop it, for pity's sake."

Anya looked at her. "Why should I pity him?"

Earth crept slowly up Macalla's throat to his chin. He struggled briefly.

"Then pity me. His death would weigh heavy on my heart."

Macalla tried to spit earth from his mouth. Saliva and mud dribbled down his chin. His eyes rolled up.

"Why?"

"Because he followed me to Dumnet when I asked it, though I broke my betrothal to him for the sake of being queen."

"You are not responsible for the path he has followed since."

"I chose to believe him about the Great Marriage instead of listening to the Mother."

"As did the king."

"Rufus doesn't hear the Mother. I do, when I listen."

The hilltop was silent but for the lazy ripple of her harp and the trickle of earth. "Reparation must be made," Anya said finally. "Are you willing to make it?"

"I am."

"Very well." She laid her palms gently across the strings. The trickle of earth became a torrent of soil that fell back down the rampart and away from Macalla. He swayed and fell. No one stepped forwards to help him. Anya put down her harp and stood. Sweat stung the new burn on her breastbone and made her hiss. Dagda had been right. She did know what to do now that the time had come.

"The price for his life is this. The Mother demands that you dedicate the rest of your life, and the life of your unborn daughter, and her daughter, and her daughter after her, to restoring the sacred stones and circles of Dumnet and tending the Brigid fire that will burn at their centre. For you, it will be a hard task; for your daughter, not so very hard. For her daughter, and the daughters after her, it will be a gift and a pleasure. And they shall give their blood to the Mother, though She will not demand pain or injury. For those who give themselves willingly to the task, there are rewards to be found and power to be gained. More than one of your daughters will be bards."

A light breeze ruffled the hilltop, moulding Airget's green robe to her legs and blowing her hair across her face. Anya crossed to Macalla and crouched down. He was still drooling. He would live, for a while, if others cut his food and reminded him to eat it. She searched the loose earth for shards of the knife and its wodeglass but found only a thin layer of grey powder, harmless now. She rubbed it into the dirt with her boot.

Beyond Macalla, Rufus was still kneeling on the turf. They had drugged him with something. She wondered how much of this night he would remember.

"Anya."

Caled stood close but did not dare to reach out and touch her. She swayed a little. This was how it would always be now.

"Can I help you?"

"Yes," she said, weary all of a sudden, tired and heartsick and lonely to her marrow. "Bring my harp."

She set off down the hillside without looking to see if he followed. He would. Here, when she spoke, others would now be too afraid to do anything but follow.

#

Anya stood by the taffrail watching the coast of Dumnet recede. Her harp and lute and drum were stowed below, in the ship's only passenger cabin. The sea was heavy and metallic under a mackerel sky.

The thin, balding man at the wheel spat over the side and cursed in Breton.

"He's not the only one glad to see the back of Dumnet," said the tall, raw-boned sailor coiling rope by the aft hatch. "Judging by the thin profit we'll make on this voyage, the captain will more than likely decide not to bother again for a while." She tossed the rope into a locker. "Of course, she never has liked Dumnet. Swears it's full of ghosts and witches." She looked at Anya. "You look like you may have an opinion on that."

Anya touched a fingertip to the healing burn on her breastbone. Like the one on her arm, it would leave a spiral-shaped scar. From the corner of her eye, she saw Vuhs sniffing at the rope locker. She took one last look at the receding coastline, then turned her back on it. "I heard many songs of many things in Dumnet," she said. "Perhaps I'll sing them for you."

"Otherwise Unremarkable"

Nicola Griffith interviewed by Nisi Shawl

If you had a different career, what would it be? (Question stolen from Ted Chiang.)

My first paid work, at the age of fifteen, was unskilled labouring (swing the pickaxe, load the wheelbarrow) on the dig of a Roman villa in North Yorkshire. I loved it—loved using my body outdoors alongside others, moving from stranger to fellow, learning to form a team. Walking two miles to the pub at night and sitting—in that boneless relaxation that comes from hard physical work—with a well-deserved pint. A later job was planting trees: digging holes, lifting, planting, filling. In between were jobs I loathed—indoors, dealing with customers of some kind. Those never lasted long—my worst was forty-five minutes. But labouring is a young, strong, healthy person's game, so as a career? Almost anything to do with the physical body, from fighting with blades, to biomechanics, to neuroscience, to the immune system and epidemiology. Evolution. Human history—the less documented the period the better because then it's all about the material culture, the physical. Living, moving—whether through space or time—things please me. If I had to choose to work on or with something not living, then perhaps something to do with water. I'm drawn to its flow, its coolth, its necessariness. I could play with water for hours—so hydrology and/or flow mechanics? Liquid—blood, beer, wine, water—fascinates me the way flame fascinates others.

Your view of writing—of living, really—is one that rejects Cartesian dualism (the separation of mental and physical existence). Please say some smart and true things about that.

Binaries are simple and so appeal to many people. But the idea is more than arrant nonsense; it is dangerous.

Consciousness is not what most of us grow up thinking it is; we are simultaneously both more and less conscious than we like to believe. I suspect "mind" or "consciousness" is a product of the body interfacing with the world. Think of the conscious mind as analogous to a car's traction—the interface of tire and asphalt, born where the rubber meets the road. There is research to show that what we think are conscious decisions are more often our bodies just acting and a split second later our minds understanding that it's happening and finding a reason for it. It all happens so fast that we confuse the order of events—perhaps because it's more comforting to feel in charge.

Who we are, what we do, how we feel and behave are all dependent upon and intertwined with our environment, physical and cultural. We do not exist without our environment, the body acting and being acted upon by the world. We are our bodies—we are what we think, what we do, how we feel. What we eat affects our mental health, as does temperature, pain, grief, sex, scent, music. Sing loud, sing long, sing with your whole body and I guarantee that if your body chemistry is not too far off kilter, you will feel brighter, lighter, more awake.

And of course when it comes to sex and gender, the notion of simple binaries is laughable.

Regarding the adventure stories you read as a child, you've said of their all-male casts: "Without women there, the men became just people." Regarding your issues with E.E. "Doc" Smith's Lensman books, you've said that their fundamental assumption is that "without men, women aren't human." Regarding Ammonite, *you've said it was written to challenge that assumption and to ask, "Are women human? Are they fully human of and by themselves—as opposed to in comparison with, or as reflections of, or warped by men?" What's the relationship between these three points?*

If we take a single subset or category of human—Black, say, or Disabled, woman, lesbian—and create a space where every single human belongs to that category, then that category can no longer function as a differentiator; it is no longer useful as either label or identity. In any such world, Black, Disabled, female and queer people are not Othered. We're the default, the Norm.

I wrote *Ammonite* to destroy those assumptions built over decades by SFF that women in and of themselves are not human, that a world of women would be insect-like (John Wyndham) unfeeling and sexless (E.E. "Doc" Smith) or vicious sexual predators who ape male behaviour (Edmund Cooper). In a world where women fill every role—generous and mean, brave and frightened, slaver and enslaved, strategic and careless, nurturing and narcissistic—a reader is forced to consider other attributes to differentiate behaviour.

This apparently made some readers very angry. The first review I saw of the book (in *Locus*) declared that although it wasn't a bad book, it lacked universal appeal, that perhaps it would have been more interesting if Marghe had had a brother. (I am not joking.) At my first reading and signing, I was accosted by a young man who wanted his money back: "You lied to me!" he said. "I bought this book under false pretences!" When I asked what he meant, he stabbed the back cover copy repeatedly, "See! Scientists and security personnel and anthropologists! Your publisher lied!" I said, "Where's the lie?" "But they're all women! How was I to know it's just about women?"

The next week, at Georgia Tech, in an English class, a student said to me, "I got about a third of the way through the book before

I realised there was no one like me in it, there were no men. For a minute I was angry, but then I realised, Wow, that must be how they—" waves at the few women students in the class "—feel every time they open a physics textbook."

You made a point of preserving your original British spellings in this book. Do you think readers notice those sorts of things?
Yes. Words are like icebergs—most of their meaning glides beneath the surface, unseen but exerting gravitational pull, and some of that meaning is only glimpsed in the brief, sharp glint of an extra u here or a second l there, reminding the reader of a word's history and heft, its unseen beginnings. Words are delicate and dangerous, their effects unpredictable: reduce them for efficiency at your peril.

Do you believe in themes? Do you consciously develop them when you write?
Themes emerge from the work. They develop naturally from a writer's own concerns as they imagine their characters, imagine a place and a circumstance, and let character and circumstance act upon each other to create story.

In our house, when we see an author consciously developing a theme, we roll our eyes and disparage it as, to use Kelley's words, "passing the theme tray." If you want to change the world, or at least sway a reader, you don't do that by drawing attention to the fact—and writing to theme does exactly that, because it makes a writer self-conscious; the reader notices. Theme needs to slip under the reader's ribs while they're not looking.

Do you believe in character arcs? Do you create them on purpose in your work?
I'm wary of almost anything described as an "arc," whether we're talking about progress, culture, history, or character. When it

comes to character what I believe in is change: the protagonist must be different at the end of the story than they were at the beginning. The character's change is what makes story; without it, fiction is just a series of events. Change of any kind—history, evolution, people—does not move in geometrically defined curves, it does not bend inevitably towards anything. Characters are people, and people don't follow arcs. We are indecisive, fragile, unpredictable. Arcs are tidy, convenient, and reassuring. Change is messier—harder to learn, harder to understand, harder to do—but more powerful.

Who and/or what lives in your back yard? I told Vonda McIntyre I saw a marmot there. Now I'm not so sure.
We live on the edge of a ravine that runs down to Carkeek Park, which runs along Puget Sound. We get a lot of wildlife. I don't think we have marmots, but you might have seen a mountain beaver—another large rodent. Once I saw what I believe was a marten, though maybe it was a fisher. We have coyotes and raccoons. Eagles, ospreys, barred owls, squirrels, voles, moles, shrews, mice, tree rats, hummingbirds—and all manner of songbirds, resident and migratory—and until we got the cats we had a family of crows who came to visit twice a day. Kelley misses them still, but I never much cared for them shitting all over the car and van.

You've been described as "an awe-inspiring visionary" and "a lovely badass." How do you see yourself, and how do you think others see you?
Until I was obviously Disabled—everyone notices people in wheelchairs and using canes, if only long enough to then deliberately look away and pretend they're not looking—I thought I was very good at not being noticed, just gliding through the crowd, drifting unseen until I chose otherwise. But the first time I said something like that to Kelley, she stared at me for a long

moment then burst out laughing. After she'd calmed down, I asked her what was so funny. At which point she laughed again and kept laughing until she was weeping and clutching herself. Eventually—it took a while, because every time she tried to talk, she'd just burst out laughing again—she said, "You're serious, aren't you? You really have no idea how people see you." And I said crossly, "They see a short-haired white woman who's obviously a dyke but otherwise unremarkable." At which point she was off again.

From Kelley's perspective, I own any room I walk into. I draw attention; people assume I'm Somebody; if I speak, people listen.

I love Kelley, and this is all very flattering, but I don't like the idea and don't want to believe it. First, I sometimes don't want to be noticed in any way. If Kelley is right, then that's impossible. I'd rather believe she's wrong. Second—and much more importantly—I learnt very early on (when I was a singer) to never, ever believe your own publicity. It's so easy—so tempting—but you cannot afford to believe it. Down that path lie all the talented and once-beloved singers and writers and actors who, perhaps, started out genuinely believing they're doing good in the world, genuinely believing that that pretty fan is, after all, only a little bit younger than they are, so where's the harm? But then because they believe what people say about their godlike talents and their amazingness and owning the room they start believing it's their right to help themselves to what they want, that in fact that young vulnerable fan truly wants what they want—of course she does—because they're so special, so who wouldn't?

No. Believing flattery is like being the fresh-faced frog hopping into a pan of water. You're twenty-two and the water you're playing in is new, cool, and delightful, but before long you're old and bloated with power, dragging dewy twenty-year-olds into your bubbling pot, being genuinely hurt and surprised when the world turns on you in disgust and calls you a monster for boiling those girls alive. But those men—and they are almost all men—made that choice right at the beginning when they chose to believe their own publicity.

Do I see myself as an "awe-inspiring visionary"? No—that sounds too like a guru or cult figure and, frankly, way too much work. Am I smart and do I sometimes connect dots other people don't? Sure, though I'm far from the only one. Do I frighten people sometimes? Yes. I am definite; that can startle people. Sometimes I can be deliberately menacing, especially where bullies are concerned. Occasionally the shock I provoke is unintentional. This doesn't happen so much anymore but I used to be prone to letting loose what I call flying monkeys: saying the unfiltered thing aloud, not stopping to think what effect the words might have. I rarely regret the sentiment but I have sometimes regretted the timing.

So do I consider myself a "badass"? No. I'm not fond of that word. Like "feisty" or "uppity," it often connotes surprise at someone of a particular age/gender/race behaving in a way considered by others to be inappropriate to their status.

And perhaps that's the key: I never did learn to behave appropriately. That is, while I (usually) know what is and is not appropriate for any given situation, what others think of me is rarely enough motivation to let "appropriateness" stop me from saying or doing what I feel is necessary or important.

I never learned the way girls and women are supposed to behave. Gender training—despite the efforts of my mother, the nuns, and my entire lower-middle-class Yorkshire upbringing—just never really stuck. I can't take credit for that; it's just how I was born, coated in sort of gender Teflon.

You often point out the importance of mirror neurons in how people receive your work: if you write vividly about a character's experience, the same neurological pathways are activated in a reader as the ones activated when they themselves have that experience. Is the presence of mirror neurons linked to possession of empathy? And can mirror neurons be excited by media other than writing—film, for instance, or music, or photography?

It's been argued that mirror neurons are the foundation of empathy. It makes sense to me that this would be so but that's not a hill I want to die on. Let me put it this way: I believe mirror neurons are necessary for empathy but not sufficient. As far as I can tell all mammals have them, and enough species of birds that I'm guessing they all do, too. It would not surprise me to discover other classes of animals do as well.

Can mirror neurons be excited by good TV and film? Of course: video is a visual medium. Though research suggests it can't do so as strongly as observing something in person, video can trigger a viewer's mirror neurons: a woman on the edge of a cliff with the wind in her face might tickle our own sensory apparatus enough for us to feel a faint echo of that wind on our own skin, if it's acted and shot well enough. But mirror neurons aren't just one set of nerves in one part of the brain; they're distributed and connected. And some studies show that in at least one area of the brain, the number of mirror neurons fired when observing a movement in real life is more than double the number that fire when watching a video of that movement. Sound can trigger mirror neurons, too, but not to the same degree as visuals, whether right there in person or virtual. Music creates emotion but does it create empathy in and of itself? I'd say no.

Triggering mirror neurons, though, is just the beginning of the kind of engagement I seek both from my readers and for myself with any book I read—what really changes a reader is immersion, the prose gripping the reader so forcibly that they cannot look away (I control the horizontal, I control the vertical . . .). You have to make the reader believe—to smell the sea, to feel the sting of the cold salt spray, to hear the gulls and feel the quayside cobbles under their feet. And then you have to make it matter, put them right there and then (cooking and starving, drinking and thinking, barely surviving and absolutely thriving . . .). Make the characters' thoughts and feelings, lessons and beliefs the reader's own—that's when they change.

You created the Twitter hashtag #CripLit. What evolved from that?
I created the hashtag to build critical mass, for community to coalesce around. With Alice Wong, I then turned it into a series of chats for anyone in the literary ecosystem—writer, editor, marketer, cover artist, poet, agent, bookseller, reviewer, playwright, serious reader—who identified as Disabled. Those chats were huge—the very first one trended on Twitter—and they were a lot of work. We ran them for two years, just me and Alice, with the occasional guest host. In those two years the needle began to move; there were stirrings in the depths in terms of how people approached Disability in literature. It had already begun in the kid lit community, but then agents began to explicitly mention criplit in their submission guidelines; calls for anthologies went out; good, serious nonfiction was being commissioned by trade presses; and here and there in various corners of the genre world crip characters were sprouting. Meanwhile, Alice and I were becoming more and more busy with other things. I hunted about briefly for some people to take over—there was real potential to form a nonprofit, a Disability-focused lit org—but one of the truisms of the Disability community is that those who do things are already doing too many things with too little energy or resources. We are all, every one, working beyond capacity. Add to

that that I'm a sprinter and spark more than a marathon runner or steady guardian of the flame. I let it go.

Would you say you are an activist?
The OED defines an activist as "an advocate of activism," and activism as a "doctrine or policy of advocating energetic action." In that Just Do It sense, yes, I'm an activist. On the other hand, Merriam-Webster defines an activist as "an especially active, vigorous advocate of a cause, especially a political cause." In this sense of committing and fighting in the trenches, of marching, phone-banking, and door-knocking, I'd have to say no. These days I'm more likely to be the one who initially points out a bias or injustice—as I did with my work on literary prize data and the bias against stories about women, or in highlighting how few Disabled voices are published—and to work to Norm the Other in my fiction.

What do you think the US government has learned from your immigration here?
Oh, ha! Ha ha ha. Governments don't learn. But people who run different bits of the government change their minds and change them back again. My immigration case made new law. The State Department declared it to be in the National Interest for me to live and work in this country and issued me a National Interest Waiver (which meant I didn't have to be married to a person of the opposite sex, didn't have to have family in the country, did not need to be in skilled employment, and didn't have to invest one million dollars in a US business)—the first time ever for an out lesbian or gay man. But then *The Wall Street Journal* got hold of the news and put me on the front page—along with one of those awful drawings—and called me a "kook" who was lowering the moral standards of the country, and within a year the National Interest Waiver programme was discontinued.

Is British English a foreign language in the US?
When I moved here, Kelley and I lived in Georgia. To many people of that state yes, English English is a foreign language. I'd say I speak Yorkshire English except, because of my parentage—mother from Yorkshire, father from London—my accent is . . . eccentric. To those who have watched PBS or listened to the BBC, who have absorbed the nuances of class and accent, it makes me sound more posh than I actually am. In this country it's a very useful accent to have in two instances: one, if you're dealing with arseholes it's a bit like whipping out a Centurion Card and having them suddenly pay attention because, hey, you might be one of those rich, powerful don't-fuck-with-me-because-I-will-fuck-back-so-much-harder gold-plated arseholes. And two—which is most of the time, especially here in Seattle—everyday people who hear my accent just assume I'm a nice neighbour who knows everything about perennial gardening and regularly has tea with the Queen.

In the tradition of Terry Bisson I'll give you three names and ask you to write just one line about each of them: Enid Blyton, Joanna Russ, Remedios Varo.
A truly terrible writer whose work I ate up as a child and without whom there would be no Earthsea, no Harry Potter, and no *The Dark Is Rising*—no cosy boarding schools for magical kids anywhere.

Brilliant, sharp, witty, and not—quite—brave enough to imagine joy.

A talented artist with a head full of spiders.

What's the first thing you know about something you write? (For me, it's the title.)
The title is always the last thing. Always. The first thing? It's impossible to generalise; I've had entire novels drop into my head

in the middle of a conference panel (*Ammonite*) or stories while walking on the beach ("Song of Bullfrogs, Cry of Geese"). Some stories or characters (Aud) appear to me in dreams. "Down the Path of the Sun" revolves around a repetitive, gut-wrenching dream I had, over and over, almost exactly the one in the story, of my little sister Helena being taken by the waves, swept away, and lost. A prophetic dream of her early death. That story—the first short story I wrote that wasn't school homework—is real and personal to me. Along with "Mirrors and Burnstone"—which was the first story I ever sold, the fourth I wrote—it was part of my submission to Clarion. And *Spear*, well, *Spear* came from a commission (for an Arthurian retelling); a refusal (No, I said, it can't be done: a story like the stories I write that still feels true to the legend? Not possible); and then an image that dropped into my head (of an exhausted person in battered bits of armour, holding a red spear, and leading a bony grey gelding through a dark wood) that made think, Oh, holy shit! I know how to make this work! But then instead of a short story I wrote a short novel. Sometimes a novel (*Slow River*) comes to me after I've bumped like a trapped bluebottle against different windows: a fascinating catalogue of industrial protective gear like eye-washing stations and neoprene suits; a vision of a spectacular, elevated glass pipeline running for miles over the desert and glittering in the sun; having sex underwater; trying to work out if there is such a thing as an essential self; and really wanting—needing—to know why I had been able to escape, (mostly) sane and (mostly) whole, the milieu I had lived in for several years while others did not. And then, in one miraculous moment, understanding that all those people, places, and impossibilities were connected . . .

They all begin in different places.

You've coedited the three anthologies in Overlook Press's series of queer-oriented speculative fiction: Bending the Landscape: Science Fiction*;* Bending the Landscape: Fantasy*; and* Bending the Landscape: Original Gay and Lesbian Horror Writing. *Are you ready to edit more books?*

Over the years I've toyed with the idea of some reprint-based project or other, but either someone else eventually comes along and does something similar or I decide it's just not as interesting as writing my own stuff. One thing I'm quite sure of: I will never edit another original anthology. Good editing (and why bother with any other kind?) is hard work. And that's just editing the prose (which does offer a measure of satisfaction). All the rest—pitching, negotiating, persuading, reading, selecting, shaping, introducing, hounding authors for signatures or bios or photos—is like trying to climb a steep muddy path with the wind howling and being blinded by flying leaves. Not fun. Not even a little bit.

Bending the Landscape, though, was a necessary project, designed to break down walls between different literary genres and cultures. I wanted straight writers to write queer characters, and literary writers to write genre stories. I solicited stories from a few people I particularly wanted but I also put out an open call. The response was an absolute tsunami: hundreds of stories for each volume. Some of the stories by new writers had something there, something buried deep, barely glimpsed, only to be guessed at. And only editing could get to it. Think Yoda raising the X-wing from the swamp. There again, he had the benefit of knowing what was there, that it was worth it; I simply had to trust my instinct that that shining thing buried deep, deep in the murk was treasure rather than an old tin, and set my will, and lift . . .

Here's an exercise you gave a Clarion West class I sat in on: Come up with a metaphor for your writing process. What's your writing process metaphor?
As I hope I said at the time, that was an exercise I learned from Kim Stanley Robinson, who asked the question of the Clarion workshop I attended in 1988. If I recall correctly, he in turn had borrowed the idea from someone who had taught him. (Damon Knight?) But memory is notoriously unreliable.

Stan told us he worked like a "blind mosaicist," feeling about for the tesserae and hoping he's putting the shapes and colours in the right places, all in service of a specific vision. One person thought of their process as Jackson Pollack–like: throw things at the canvas and see what happens. Many compared writing to making music: composing, playing, conducting. But while musicality is inherent in my own work—in the beat and rhythm of it—for me writing is much more visceral. If I had to choose one metaphor then it would be sculpture—everything from carving rich, fine-grained wood to taking hammer and chisel to granite to the furious speed and heat of blowing and twisting glass. Writing can be either muscle and bone—stone dust and sawdust and glass fumes, sweat and gargantuan effort—or slow patience—delicate, exacting, precise. Often, it is both: see a massive cube of stone and jackhammer off chunks, consider; switch to mallet and chisel, consider; pick up a small file . . . Or choose a beautiful chunk of wood, something I want to cradle in my hands, feel its heft and warmth, plane it down, let the knots and grain guide the shape. Taking away every single piece that doesn't belong until you have a shape that can be nothing but itself, a self made plain, right there.

Writing is not the only art you practice—this book includes three of your drawings. What can you tell people about "Griffin, Maybe," "King Bird," *and* "Happy Hound"*?*

I use an iPad Pro and Pencil for historical research, pulling up and annotating by hand PDFs; drawing timelines; sketching maps. Handwriting is a much more direct connection to the creative mind than a keyboard—literally more hands-on, more visceral. The maps began as a way to work out battle scenes for *Hild* and *Menewood* but soon became a meditative act—a way of wandering, untethered, into my imagination without having to leave the house. For those maps I needed little icons to represent various leaders or battles. Animal totems were the obvious choice, so I researched Early Medieval art. I was struck by the strong sense of graphic design in illuminated manuscripts like the *Lindisfarne Gospels*, and itched to try my hand. These pieces are part of a larger project, a challenge I set myself to work only in black and white within a circle. All three are inspired by (but in actual fact not very much like) images from the eighth-century *Book of Kells*. My hound, for example, probably wasn't originally meant to represent a hound. It had no ears, and it certainly didn't have that goofy grin!

Please ask yourself a question I failed to ask you. Then answer it.

"What attributes does a writer need?"

You must be brave. You need an almost psychotic self-belief. I've said elsewhere that being a writer sometimes feels like being a shaman—you have to wander into the unknown.

But how can you tell when you're following your star to undiscovered country and when you're just wandering the woods, ranting and lost? It can be a tenuous distinction, and never more so than at the beginning.

Beginning feels a little like hearing a voice or glimpsing a shape in the mist, and, with no rational hope for success—only the sudden sense that it's important, it's necessary, it might just be magic—leaping up and flinging yourself into the void in pursuit.

Sometimes there's a moment when you find yourself alone on the moor with the mist rising and night falling, and behind you the door back to reality is closing . . .

I've learnt to tell when a shape in the mist is real and when it's just an echo, something insubstantial that will vanish on contact, or a misbegotten monster that will torment you for years. I can't tell you how I know the difference; perhaps this is the central mystery of creativity. A wordless knowing. A thing of the body. But in the end, you have to take that leap. You have to be brave.

About the Author

Nicola Griffith was born in Leeds, Yorkshire, England. At seventeen she went to the University of Leeds to study microbiology and biochemistry but dropped out after a few months and moved to Hull, where she fronted a band, Janes Plane. She has studied several martial arts and taught women's self-defence until not long before her MS diagnosis in 1993. In 1988 she attended the Clarion Writers Workshop at Michigan State University, where she met fellow writer Kelley Eskridge; in 1989 she moved to the US so they could be together. The couple were married in 1993, though the marriage was not legally recognised. Griffith became a dual UK/US citizen in spring of 2013. Later that year, on the twentieth anniversary of their original ceremony, she and Eskridge were legally married.

Griffith's first literary award was a BBC North poetry prize for a piece submitted without her knowledge by a teacher. Her first professionally published story was "Mirrors and Burnstone," in the UK magazine *Interzone* (1988).

Since 1993 and the publication of her debut novel *Ammonite*, which won the James Tiptree Jr. (now Otherwise) Award, Griffith has been the recipient of over twenty literary awards for her work, including multiple Lambda Literary and Washington State Book awards, and has been a finalist for many others.

In 2015 Griffith published a statistical survey of bias in the literary prize ecosystem showing that stories about women did not win the most prestigious literary prizes. The data went viral and she was interviewed on four continents. Many others took the work forwards, applying the statistical approach to various genres, and the $50,000 Half the World Global Literati Prize was established as a direct result.

Griffith began using a wheelchair in 2016. In 2017 she earned a PhD By Published Work from Anglia Ruskin University. She has served as a board trustee for a variety of nonprofit boards such as the Lambda Literary Foundation and the Multiple Sclerosis Association. In 2024, she was inducted into the Science Fiction and Fantasy Hall of Fame at the Museum of Popular Culture, and in 2025 was named as SFWA's 41st Damon Knight Memorial Grand Master.

FRIENDS OF

These are indisputably momentous times—the financial system is melting down globally and the Empire is stumbling. Now more than ever there is a vital need for radical ideas.

In the years since its founding—and on a mere shoestring—PM Press has risen to the formidable challenge of publishing and distributing knowledge and entertainment for the struggles ahead. With hundreds of releases to date, we have published an impressive and stimulating array of literature, art, music, politics, and culture. Using every available medium, we've succeeded in connecting those hungry for ideas and information to those putting them into practice.

Friends of PM allows you to directly help impact, amplify, and revitalize the discourse and actions of radical writers, filmmakers, and artists. It provides us with a stable foundation from which we can build upon our early successes and provides a much-needed subsidy for the materials that can't necessarily pay their own way. You can help make that happen—and receive every new title automatically delivered to your door once a month—by joining as a Friend of PM Press. And, we'll throw in a free T-shirt when you sign up.

Here are your options:

- $30 a month: Get all books and pamphlets plus 50% discount on all webstore purchases
- $40 a month: Get all PM Press releases (including CDs and DVDs) plus 50% discount on all webstore purchases
- $100 a month: Superstar—Everything plus PM merchandise, free downloads, and 50% discount on all webstore purchases

For those who can't afford $30 or more a month, we have Sustainer Rates at $15, $10, and $5. Sustainers get a free PM Press T-shirt and a 50% discount on all purchases from our website.

Your Visa or Mastercard will be billed once a month, until you tell us to stop. Or until our efforts succeed in bringing the revolution around. Or the financial meltdown of Capital makes plastic redundant. Whichever comes first.

PM Press is an independent, radical publisher of critically necessary books for our tumultuous times. Our aim is to deliver bold political ideas and vital stories to all walks of life and arm the dreamers to demand the impossible. Founded in 2007 by a small group of people with decades of publishing, media, and organizing experience, we have sold millions of copies of our books, most often one at a time, face to face. We're old enough to know what we're doing and young enough to know what's at stake. Join us to create a better world.

PM Press
PO Box 23912
Oakland, CA 94623
info@pmpress.org

PM Press in Europe
europe@pmpress.org
www.pmpress.org.uk